Marie Antoinette
and
The Hidden Door of Versailles

Marie Antoinette and The Hidden Door of Versailles

Website: terilreynolds.com
The author is known as *TeriGigi* on YouTube, Instagram, Twitter and Pinterest.

Marie Antoinette and The Hidden Door of Versailles is the author's imaginative story built around actual events. Besides well-known people, locations, and circumstances that are the framework in which the story takes place, there are also made up characters and locations as well. Any similarities to current events or living persons are purely unintentional.

Typesetting and cover design: FormattingExperts.com

ISBN 978-0-692-05182-5
Library of Congress Control Number: 2017919559
Feather Light Publishing

Marie Antoinette
and
The Hidden Door of Versailles

TERI L. REYNOLDS

This book is dedicated to my husband Scott

I will never forget our first visit to Versailles on that cool, overcast October day. Things were going well until I decided we should forgo the tram, and instead, walk over to Marie Antoinette's Hamlet. I've always wanted to visit the French countryside, but that day was one for the record books. I'm not sure how many miles we walked through the woods, hopelessly lost, but I do remember that moment of elation when we saw a glimpse of the palace through the trees right before sunset. We had made it back!

Without agreeing to take me to Paris all those years ago, and many times since, I would've never been inspired to write this novel. Thank you for being so patient and supportive throughout this process.

I'm so glad Paris is "our thing." The memories are endless...

Nous aurons toujours Paris.
Teri

Dauphin
The heir apparent to the French throne

Dauphine
The wife of the heir apparent to the French throne

Prologue
The Carriage Ride

November, 1789

Inside the carriage the two men were jostled back and forth as they traveled down the deserted muddy road. The constant steady drizzle made the journey slow and difficult.

"The weather is turning," said the young man, glancing at the ominous sky in the distance. "Tell me again, why we are going all the way out there? What are you looking for?"

The older man let out a sigh. "I told you, I wish to examine it for myself. I desire to see if there is anything of significance left."

"Word has it that nothing remains. Everything was stolen or destroyed by the mob."

"It's the end of an era my young friend. I want a piece of it, a trinket, to have as a symbol of what we've accomplished so far. The result of the rebellion is the biggest triumph in the history of our country."

"Yes... but they still live."

"Not for long. Not if I have any say in the matter."

The young man grimaced at his friend's menacing tone. The future remained uncertain, for all.

Part I

Chapter 1

Marie's eyes flew open. Her body trembled, fear caught in her throat almost suffocating her. *What is it? What's happening?* Darting her eyes around the room she saw nothing. No light came in around the edges of the thick drapes covering the windows. The darkness was complete, oppressive.

She reached over to be reassured by Louis' presence but found his side of the bed empty. *He must have retired to his bedchamber sometime during the night,* she thought. She rose from the bed and reached for the crystal pitcher and glass that were kept on her nightstand. The pitcher was icy to the touch and she shivered when the cold water slid down the back of her throat. She glanced over to the fireplace and saw that the fire had died down. *I need an extra coverlet.* She opened a small door next to her bed that led into her private dressing room. As she stepped across the threshold, the chandelier behind her tinkled ever so slightly, and at the same moment, a queer sensation cut through her body. She hesitated, and then quickly returned to bed. Unable to shake the uneasiness in her spirit she rolled over and pulled the heavy covers tightly around her. She exhaled slowly, and within moments, fell back into a deep sleep.

Waking up hours later, she immediately sensed something wasn't quite right. Furrowing her brows, yet remaining perfectly still, it suddenly hit her—the smell. The air smelled stale, musty, very unlike the pungent odor that Versailles usually had.

She sat up in bed wondering where the odor originated. The room was still dark, but tiny slits of light peeked out from around the drapes. She wondered why her courtiers had not come in to wake her. They were usually present when she woke, bustling about getting ready for her morning dressing ritual. As much as she wanted to linger in her unexpected privacy, the odd smell had her curious. She climbed out of bed, padded over to one of the massive floor-to-ceiling windows and threw open the drapes. The estate was covered in a dense fog, unlike any she had seen before. Squinting, she perceived changes in the landscape, but the fog made it difficult for her to see clearly.

Turning back toward her bed, she froze. Her hand-carved writing desk was gone, along with the quill and inkwell she had used to pen a letter to her mother just the night before. The left corner of the room was bare, no longer holding her golden harp and stool, or her music stand. Her treasured harpsichord was missing as well. She quickly scanned the rest of the room. Paintings surrounding her bed appeared dull and lifeless. There was no fire in the fireplace and the soot that usually stained the underside of the mantel was gone. One lone object stood on the mantel: an unfamiliar clock. Nothing was as it had been when she and Louis had retired to bed the night before.

She hurried across the dimly lit room toward her dressing area, feeling for the hidden door which was cleverly covered with ornate gilded wallpaper that perfectly matched the walls of the room. She flung the door open and peered inside. Everything was gone—clothes, shoes, hats, brushes and combs, even her priceless jewelry collection. Only a chaise and an empty side table remained. *Where are my things? What has happened?*

Panic set in as she pulled her thin cotton dressing gown closer around her tiny frame and in her bare feet raced through a series of the back hallways that connected her room to Louis', calling out to him as she went. Breaking protocol, she flung the door open. He was not there, and his room was in a similar condition to hers. She hurried into the next room, and the next and the next. The palace was almost bare. Lifeless. Haunting. It had been robbed of its grandeur; only a shell remained.

She glanced out the windows of each room as she searched. The fog lingered. She didn't expect to see any of the gardeners due to the weather, and indeed she did not. In fact, she saw no one at all. Approaching the center wing of the palace and looking out onto the outer courtyard, she could barely make out the enormous golden gate and fence that separated the palace from the outside world. Again, she saw no one.

She began running through the many hallways and corridors searching, but not seeing or hearing anyone. Periodically she called out, but received no answer. She dashed through the Hall of Mirrors darting her eyes back and forth, her own reflection seeming to chase after her. The massive chandeliers hung in their original places, unlit, but something else caught her eye. The top of each candle was enclosed in tear shaped glass. *That's odd*, she thought, and quickly she continued on.

Marie paused a moment when she entered the Royal Chapel where she had been married a few years earlier. Although the room was empty, the walls and ceiling retained their original opulence. She glanced up at the elegantly painted ceiling. Heavenly bodies stared down at her the same way they always had at daily mass. Tears stung her eyes and she began crying out of fear and frustration. *Did thieves come in during the night and take everything? Where is everyone? Over a thousand people live and work at Versailles every day. Where are they now?*

Chapter 2

Marie collapsed onto a cold metal chair, exhausted. She had done a quick search through the main rooms of the center, north, and south wings of the chateau. Everything was different. Many treasured items were gone, moved, or changed. Entire rooms had been rearranged. Even more disturbing were the new things that had appeared, items she didn't recognize or understand. Furthermore, she had yet to find another human being. She had never been alone in her entire life, having left her family's palace in Austria at the age of 14 to travel to Versailles for an arranged marriage to Louis XVI, heir to the throne. At some point in the future she would become queen of France. Members of the court surrounded her daily, so much so, that she rarely had a moment to herself. Now, alone and confused, she felt numb.

The palace was completely abandoned, but she had not yet searched the grounds. Immediately making her way out to the vast gardens, she looked left, right, and down toward the fountains and the man-made lakes in the distance. Still, she saw no one.

Quickly descending the massive steps, almost sprinting at times, she searched the grounds finding them not only abandoned, but like the palace, stripped of the elegance and beauty they once held. Everywhere she looked was a dressed-down version of the original. As she continued searching, she kept a constant watch all around her, sometimes spinning in circles. The fog made her extremely anxious and she couldn't shake the feeling she was being watched. Although desperate to find someone, anyone, her senses were on high alert. *What if there are thieves and they are still here? Who will protect me?*

Continuing onward through the dense fog, she could barely make out the Apollo fountain in the distance, but as she got closer she noticed the horses and figures had a dull patina to them, and the silent, still water made them seem frozen in time.

Further ahead she saw an unfamiliar dark green building surrounded by tables and chairs. As she approached, she noticed a menu board hanging in the front window, and around the back of the building, she was surprised to find an unlocked door. Opening it slowly and cautiously, she entered a room full of strange objects. Along the back wall was a large box with a glass door and behind the glass were clear bottles, which according to the labels were filled with water. She opened the door and picked one up expecting it to be made of glass, but it was much lighter and thinner, and gave way slightly when she gripped it. She put the bottle back, and noticed a baguette and wheel of Brie on the counter. Despite her hunger, she left the food untouched.

On the opposite wall, sitting on another counter, was an unusual metal box. She tentatively pulled down a knob on the side, and jumped back when with a ding, a hidden drawer opened unexpectedly. The drawer was full of money and coins unlike any she had ever seen. *It's a strongbox,* she thought, eyeing its contents curiously. She pushed the drawer closed and exited the building.

Looking left, she noticed a small octagon-shaped structure painted the same green color with a TOILETTE sign in front of it. Carefully opening the door marked Madame, she entered a small room containing a toilet and a sink. She had never seen such a toilet, yet out of necessity decided to make use of it, as she hadn't relieved herself since waking up. When finished, she rose to leave and a loud whooshing sound startled her. Looking back, she was shocked to find water rushing down a hole, and just as quickly, it was replaced with clear, clean water. Walking over to the sink, she examined it carefully. As her hand neared the spout, water began flowing. As she moved her hand away, the water stopped. Tilting her head in confusion, she turned and left.

Exhausted from her search, she began slowly walking back to the palace, with each step, becoming more and more agitated that the palace guards had abandoned her. *How dare they leave me,* she thought. *This is unacceptable!* The idea that she could be in a strange dream crossed her mind, but she knew deep down inside she wasn't dreaming. It was all too real, even if it defied explanation. It began to drizzle so she hurried back inside the palace, escaping the elements.

Moving across the black and white marble floor, she entered the main receiving room that opened out to the front courtyard. It was a large room where visitors to the chateau would be received upon arrival. It looked completely different now. On a large, long wooden table in the center of the room, she saw stacks of folded maps printed in many different languages. *Maps of the palace? How odd.* She continued around the room, observing but not understanding. Her eyes rested on a calendar on the far wall. Fear descended. The month at the top of the calendar was November, but the year was more than 200 years into the future. *That isn't right! The year is 1773!*

Dropping into one of the simple wooden chairs, her heart raced. She clutched her chest, her breaths coming in rapid succession. *What does this mean?* Fearing she would pass out, she sprang to her feet, not sure what to do. Panicked, she ran—ran right out of the palace across the cobblestone courtyard and onto the gravel expanse all the way to the enormous front gate. She shook the gate violently trying to open it, the metal clanging loudly. It was locked tight. Fingers slowly sliding down the cold slender bars, she crumpled to the ground weeping uncontrollably. The rain continued to fall, soaking her nightgown. *I—don't understand. What is the meaning? What do I...* With sobs racking her body, she did not hear the man approach.

Chapter 3

"Mademoiselle, may I help you?"

Marie stiffened. She slowly lifted her head. Raindrops mixed with tears made it difficult for her to see. Standing on the other side of the golden fence was a tall bearded man dressed in a heavy black overcoat. She remained perfectly still. Raindrops continued to blur her vision, but as the figure moved his hand through the fence, she jumped up and ran. Halfway, she stumbled and fell, skidding across the gravel, but somehow made it back inside the palace, slamming the massive door behind her. With her back against the door she tried to calm herself. *Why did he frighten me so? Why did I run?* Desperate to find someone to help her, she instantly regretted her actions.

Still afraid but curious, she crawled to the nearest window and cautiously stretched her neck to peek out. The man in black was still there, although she could barely make out his silhouette through the condensation on the glass. He shook the gate back and forth, peered through the bars, and finally walked on. His body changed shape as she watched him through the rivers of rain dripping down the warped glass, but she noticed he had a slight limp. Once more he glanced back. *Shall I call out to him?* Her instinct said no, but as she watched her only hope disappear into the fog, her indecision gave way to a new sense of hopelessness. But she now knew there were others, just beyond the protection of the palace gates.

Exhausted and weary, she decided to get out of her wet gown and lie down. Walking slowly toward her bedchamber, she noticed a door off to one side, again marked TOILETTE. She went inside to the sink, placing her hands under the spout as she had done before. Her cold hands stung as she carefully picked out the tiny gravel bits that were imbedded in her palms from the fall. Lifting her legs one at a time over the side of the sink allowed her to rinse her muddy feet. She shivered as she walked down the corridor, leaving behind tiny damp footprints with each step.

Once back in her room she felt better. She removed her soaked nightgown and laid it out to dry on the end of her bed. As she crawled between the sheets, she noticed that the bedding was different and the mattress felt much firmer than usual. Not understanding any of this, she tried to adjust her body into a comfortable position. Soon her frustration grew and she pounded her fist into an unfamiliar pillow and began sobbing. *Where is everyone? Why is Versailles the same, and yet so different? That calendar...*

Questions swirled through her mind and her anxiety grew as she tossed and turned. *Calm down, compose yourself,* she thought, *be strong.* Rolling over once more, she felt something pricking her side. She reached down and found her rosary, the one she had clutched between her fingers before falling asleep the night before. She wrapped the familiar chain around her palm and gripped the cross in her fist. Naked and shivering, she drew the covers tight and began reciting prayers she had learned as a child. Her mind spent, she finally fell asleep, hoping that when she woke the world she once knew would have returned. In her dreams, she was back in her childhood home in Austria, running from room to room searching—for what, she did not know.

Late in the afternoon she slowly awoke, her heart sinking when she found her surroundings the same. The air outside was colder, still a mixture of mist and fog. *How strange to have the fog last throughout the day*. It certainly added a sense of doom to her already forlorn spirit. She sat up in bed feeling lost, wondering how long she could remain in the silent, empty palace.

Her stomach growled. For the first time in her young life she had to take charge, do things for herself. She decided to return to the green building to gather some bread and cheese. She donned her still damp nightgown and returned to the reception room where earlier she had noticed some bags and coats in a closet marked OBJECTS TROUVÉ (Lost and Found). After gathering a large leather satchel, a camel-colored wool coat, and a pair of leather boots carelessly tossed in the corner, she dared to look out toward the front gate. No, he was not there.

Once back at the green shack, she stocked her bag full of bread, cheese, and some of the water bottles. She would figure out how to open them later. It was all so unfamiliar, yet it amazed her how quickly her mind found acceptance of all the strange and puzzling things that were happening to her as she focused on survival. As an afterthought, she pushed the buttons on the brass box on the counter, and when it opened, she took out all the money, acknowledging an unfamiliar pang of guilt from taking something that did not belong to her. She had never had to take anything. Everything was always given to her.

Slowly walking the long pathway back to the palace, Marie returned to her room and sat down in the one lone chair positioned between the windows, ignoring the sign above it that read NE PAS S'ASSEOIR (Do Not Sit). She found peace and comfort in the surroundings of her room. Even though it now felt cavernous and uninviting, at least it was hers.

As night fell, she crawled back into bed. She periodically heard the faint sound of distant rolling thunder, once thinking it was the echo of horses' hooves approaching. The palace was completely dark. Most the candles and candlesticks were gone, and there was no wood for a fire. She felt isolated, alone, abandoned. As her eyes adjusted, she noticed a red glow in the room. Sitting up and leaning forward, there, over the doorway was a glowing sign, which read SORTIE (Exit). Exhaling, she knew this was but another strange object she didn't understand.

Gradually the rain stopped, the clouds parted, and soft moonlight streamed in the windows reflecting off the gold gilt around the room. The ornamental angels carved into the crown molding above her bed stared down at her. She contemplated her situation with a mixture of fear and resolve. In the morning, as soon as the sun rose, she would gather her bag with her provisions, put the coat on over her nightclothes, and leave Versailles.

Chapter 4

Early the next morning the sun cascaded through the open drapes into Marie's bedroom. As she stirred, she instantly felt uneasy. In her sleepy state she couldn't remember why. Slowly opening her eyes and looking around the bare room, the shock of all that she had discovered the day before came rushing back to her. She seemed to be in the future, yet had no idea how it happened, or if it was even real. Her plan to leave Versailles was set in her mind last night, but this morning it seemed risky. Her confidence was gone.

As she raised her hand to wipe away a tear that threatened to spill over, her rosary dangled from her wrist sending starbursts of diamond reflections all around the room. She unwrapped it from her hand and put it around her neck. She rubbed the delicate gold cross between her fingers. Her mother's words as she left home to come to France echoed in her mind. "Be strong Antonia, do not let them see you as weak." Although these words were spoken under different circumstances, they had left their mark. With renewed strength she rose up, tied the coat around her, slipped on the boots, grabbed the leather bag and struck out toward the front of the palace.

As she walked along the wide hallway, she saw something she had not noticed in her panic the day before. Along the wall standing under one of the many paintings was a pedestal with a small plaque on it. The plaque was engraved, LOUIS XV (1710-1774). *1774!* The implication hit her hard. *The king will die next year?* She and Louis would become king and queen much sooner than they expected. *It can't be!* She looked up at the massive painting, staring into the eyes of the king. Confused and perplexed she hurried along the corridor. She stopped suddenly, her heart skipping a beat, when quite unexpectedly she heard voices!

Quickly jumping behind a door, she held her breath and felt the hair on her neck standing up and her heart beating rapidly. Two men walked toward her. "We are supposed to remove that huge tapestry in the War Room and send it out for cleaning. It's such a bitch to get on and off the wall."

"Let's just say we did it. Who cares?"

Marie could not believe her ears. *Who cares? Everyone cares about Versailles!*

"You know Brigette, she'll have our hide if she finds out."

"Okay, okay. Let's get the ladder from the basement. We've got to get it down and out before the doors open for the day."

She peeked out from behind the door. The men were dressed in plain dark clothing, very unlike the dress of her time. Her heart was beating so loudly she felt certain they would hear, but they took no notice of her as they passed. *There are others in the palace! Where did they come from?* She made her way from room to room, careful to remain hidden. Periodically, she noticed other people focused on their tasks.

Each time she heard someone approaching, she hid. She was able to hide quite easily, the palace being so familiar to her. In court life, the constant presence of people could be suffocating and she had learned quickly where she could duck away, if only for a moment. The palace was full of secret passageways and hidden rooms. Her memory served her well and the closer she got to the reception room, the louder the voices became behind the walls.

She quietly crept up a concealed staircase, walked along a hidden corridor, and peered out a set of massive arched windows. What she saw took her breath away. In the front outer courtyard were hundreds of people walking across the cobblestones, forming long lines. They all seemed to be waiting to come inside. They wore coats similar to the one she wore from the reception room closet. She hoped to get outside among them without being recognized or noticed.

Walking further along, still carrying her heavy bag of food and water, she crept down yet another set of stairs that led out to a back walkway to the carriage house. She moved along silently and peered in one of the carriage house windows, and indeed, it was full of carriages, including the one that originally had brought her from Austria to Versailles years ago.

Coming around the corner of the building, she hesitated for only a moment, then bravely stepped out of concealment and blended into the crowd. She dared not speak to anyone. *Too risky* she thought. She heard numerous languages as she made her way through the crowd, but it was difficult to hear their private conversations. She was glad her blonde hair was down, long and straight. It wasn't a style she would ever normally wear, but now it allowed her to blend in easily. Her nightgown peeked out from under the long coat, but only a bit. As she walked, her body trembled to the point she was afraid she wouldn't be able to keep her balance. She kept her head down, careful not to make eye contact with anyone. Even though she wanted to ask questions, seek help, she thought it best not to draw attention to herself until she could learn more.

She easily walked right out through the open palace gates, which had been shut tight the day before, and made her way along the wide path. The town of Versailles had grown. Instead of the buildings being a respectful distance away, they were now built right up to the edge of the palace fence. Being the only person walking away from the palace rather than toward it, she stepped down off the curb and stood in the street wondering which way to go.

Without warning, a loud sound made her turn, and she saw a large and terrifying object racing toward her. She stood frozen, mouth open, mesmerized by the object. The sound it made was deafening. At the last moment, it swerved and a voice from inside yelled at her to get out of the way. Marie sprinted over to a stand of trees and crouched in the bushes, shaking violently. More of the strange devices traveled up and down the road without the aid of horses. Bewildered, she considered returning to the palace, but once her breathing slowed and she realized that neither the objects, nor the people inside were after her, she decided to carry on.

She stepped out from among the trees and continued walking, carefully avoiding the street as more and more of the strange objects traveled at great speeds past her. A few of the buildings she saw vaguely matched the architecture of her time, but there were others that did not. She walked on, turning this way and that. How odd it felt to walk alone, unnoticed. She never did anything without being noticed since she had come to live in France. Everything she said or did, even the clothes she wore, were a topic of discussion. As dauphine, and someday queen, all eyes were constantly on her. Now, everything was different. It was as if she were invisible. This sense of anonymity made her feel safer and bolder. No one knew who she was, and oddly, no one seemed to care.

She turned a corner and across the street stood a building marked, GARE (Railway Station). *What is this place?* She watched from a distance as people come in and out of the building, some of them carrying large cases. She watched as others stood on different corners of the intersection, and from time to time, when the moving objects stopped, the people crossed the road safely. Timidly she walked over and stood next to two women, and when they stepped into the street, she followed closely behind them and made it safely to the other side.

Once in front of the building, she stood on her tiptoes to look in the windows and see what was inside. It was one large room with very high ceilings. People were everywhere milling about, some sitting, some standing, but mostly people were coming back and forth through some sort of moving gate. She decided to get a closer look.

She waited until no one was near and walked over to the entrance. As soon as she reached the door, it magically opened in front of her. Then the door to her left magically opened too, and she stood amazed as 2 men exited the building. Suddenly a woman and child came up behind her and the woman said, "Well, are you going in or not?" Marie quickly walked through the doorway and rushed over to her right and stood along the wall. She had made it inside.

The place was crowded and confusing. The back wall of the room was mostly glass, so she could see as people walked through the back doorway and stepped into a series of long, blue and white cylinder shaped chambers. She could see people inside, looking out toward the station through long rows of windows. A minute passed by and the entire series of chambers slowly moved forward, picked up speed, and disappeared from sight. *A multiple carriage apparatus? Utterly fantastic!*

She turned her attention back to the room, and over to the left she noticed a chart on the wall titled, BILLETS DE TRAIN. *Train ticket? Is this thing called a train?* Then she saw it. Printed right there before her eyes: PARIS. *Is this a way to get to Paris? Do I dare?*

A quick decision was made before she could talk herself out of it. She would leave and go to Paris. *Perhaps the present royal family could be located there. Obviously, they no longer rule from Versailles. Maybe I can have an audience with the king, and ask for help.*

Chapter 5

Marie knew Paris well having traveled there several times. She had been officially presented to the Parisian citizens just months ago at the Tuileries Palace with much fanfare. They were eager to see the dauphine. The introduction had gone well. Now she would be traveling back to Paris, only this time, under very different circumstances.

Stepping back, she stood along the wall of the station wondering what to do next. *Will this "train" take me to Paris?* She observed a young woman who approached a small window and said, "Ticket to Paris," and handed over money like the money she took from the green building back in the gardens. The woman was then handed a small paper tag. The schedule on the wall read: DÉPART PARIS 9:15.

Marie looked at the large clock hanging next to the schedule. *Only ten minutes until departure,* she thought. Taking a deep breath she approached the ticket window, she simply said, "Ticket to Paris." Handing the clerk a bill, she was given some coins in return, along with a small paper tag. She glanced over just as the young woman inserted her tag into a slot, and went through the turning gate. Marie followed suit and continued behind the young woman, right out the doorway and up the steps onto the train. She took a seat and placed her bag on the floor next to her feet, waiting for what was to come. Despite the knot in her stomach, she felt a small sense of accomplishment; she was braver than she thought. Though she was used to having absolutely everything done for her, now she was thinking for herself, being resourceful. *All I need to do is imitate the others.* If she could continue her keen sense of observation, she felt she would be all right until she could return to her former life. She had no idea how she would return, but her sense of duty demanded it.

Sitting perfectly still, Marie glanced out the window watching as the last few passengers boarded the train. She was trying to appear normal, but was careful to avoid eye contact, or even worse, conversation.

Suddenly out of the corner of her eye she saw a man dressed in a long black overcoat standing on the platform. He was looking up and down the walkway, craning his neck to see as far as possible. He raised his eyes, which were shadowed by the brim of his hat, and immediately he saw her. An eerie feeling washed over her as they locked eyes. At that moment the train began slowly moving forward, but he did not take his eyes off her. His gaze was unsettling, intense. Looking down to adjust her bag at her feet, she felt frightened, uneasy. She thought he could be the same man she saw at the gates of the palace the day before, but she couldn't be sure. He seemed to recognize her, to know her. As the train cleared the platform, she cautiously looked back. He had vanished.

Relief came over her that he was gone, but as the train picked up speed, she became frightened at the sensation and held on tightly to the back of the seat in front of her. Slowly, she became accustomed to the movement and the unfamiliar sounds coming from the train. *It's certainly much smoother than carriage travel,* she thought, her mind flashing back to other journeys she had made to Paris, being jostled back and forth on the bumpy, sometimes muddy roads. She began to relax, if only a bit, despite thinking occasionally of the man in black.

Paris was usually a half a day's ride by carriage, so she was shocked when she saw the city coming into view within 30 minutes of leaving Versailles. Her heart sank. It had certainly changed; in fact, the city was barely recognizable.

Marie began to feel the nerves crawl up her spine again, knowing she would soon have to get off the train. Stop after stop went by, yet she sat motionless in her seat, wondering when she would have the courage to disembark. As the train slowed to approach the next stop, she noticed a sign outside the window that read, ST-MICHEL/NOTRE DAME. *Notre Dame*! A familiar place—a place she knew! She quickly exited the train once it slowed to a stop, hoping to find the church she had been to before, as dauphine.

She left the station, carefully following the signs directing her to the Cathedral. Paris had been transformed. Gone was the horrible stench she had grown accustomed to, but other unfamiliar odors were equally unpleasant. The city was clean and well swept, other than an occasional bit of paper drifting by in the breeze. The same moving objects she encountered in Versailles moved along the roads swiftly, only now there were many more. She stayed out of their way, but the roaring sounds they made bombarded her senses.

Walking swiftly along, she felt safe and discreet. As before, no one seemed to notice her or really care about her presence. She wondered if she would ever get used to being ignored. It wasn't long until Notre Dame came into view in all its original glory. She uttered a whimper, so happy she was to see something standing as it stood hundreds of years ago. The church was the same, and yet the surrounding area was totally different. She walked the perimeter of the cathedral, but didn't dare enter, not sure why she hesitated. Toward the back of the building, she gazed up at the flying buttresses that fascinated her now, as they did before in her other life. It seemed the people of this time period found it fascinating as well. They were everywhere, sitting, walking, standing, and constantly raising small boxes up to their eyes. Marie wasn't sure what the boxes were, but she guessed it was some sort of telescope used to get a closer look.

Not sure what to do next, she sat down on a bench in a small park located at the back of the church. Just to her left, she saw the Seine. It was beautiful as the sunlight shimmered on the water, so different from the dirty, smelly river of the 18th century. Looking up and down the river, bridge after bridge was laid out before her. She was amazed how much had changed in 200 years. Paris was certainly much larger, and the common people seemed more civilized, orderly and purposeful in their manner, even if their way of dress was appalling.

She continued walking, eager to see what else was still standing from her time. She crossed over the Pont d'Arcole and carefully walked along the Seine, dodging people as she went, seeing signs that pointed her to The Musee de Louvre. *The Louvre is still standing, but is now a museum? What has happened?*

Walking on the sidewalk along the side of the Louvre, she felt as comforted by its familiarity as she had been by Notre Dame. She walked the entire length of the palace not seeing an entrance until coming to the far end, and was quickly caught up in a crowd of people moving in mass toward the building. Rounding the corner, she was shocked to see so much empty space. *Where is the Tuileries Palace?* Instead, there was a huge expanse of bright green grass in front of the Louvre where the Tuileries once stood. Her heart sank. She had imagined she might be able to reach the present royal family at the palace and receive hospitality.

She was pulled along with the crowd and was soon inside the enormous courtyard area. It was open, filled with the sky. She was sure this area once held more of the palace's structures, but now she saw only a few fountains, and two stunning glass pyramids standing amongst them. People were entering one of the glass pyramids and disappearing underground. *Where might this lead?* Following the others, thinking she could pause and assess the situation once inside, she was immediately fed onto a moving staircase going straight down. It was terrifying and exhilarating at the same time. She gripped the moving handrail until the tips of her fingers ached. She nearly tripped at the bottom but managed to keep her balance. Marie was now standing in the middle of a vast atrium, sunlit from above, full of people going off in all directions to different parts of the building.

She quickly made her way to a small marble bench off to the side out of the confusion. She needed to catch her breath and calm her anxious spirit. Breathing deeply as she rocked back and forth a bit, she noticed two things that greatly interested her, an arrow leading to the toilettes, and the smell of food. Her stomach growled. It was now past lunchtime, and she had only had a bit of bread while on the train.

She followed a group of ladies to the expansive restroom. Peeking into one of the many stalls, she was relieved to find it just like the ones at Versailles. Once finished, she stood and waited. The water didn't whoosh away this time. She shrugged, exited the stall and walked over to the sinks. She peered into the mirror in front of her, and was shocked at her appearance, embarrassed that she had been walking around the city looking so unkempt. Rinsing her face and smoothing her hair carefully, she exited the bathroom.

She walked across the atrium toward the smell of food and noticed a huge glass case filled with sandwiches, fruit, and desserts. Although desperately wanting to partake, Marie instead sat at a table alone and ate some of the now stale bread and cheese from her bag, all the while taking in her surroundings. Soon she relaxed, realizing again, she was anonymous.

Up ahead was a large hall lined with shops, and at the end, an exit. She decided to go over to that area and have a look around. Rising from the table she made her way once again across the sunlit atrium.

The first shop she came to was an enormous bookstore. The tall bookshelves were polished to a high sheen and the area smelled of fine wood. Walking around the shop, she was awestruck by the rows and rows of books in their colorful book-jackets, very unlike the plain cloth or leather bound books she was used to. She wandered over to the "French History" section, fascinated by some of the titles. One in particular caught her attention immediately, "*The French Monarchy... From the Sun*

King to the Revolution 1643-1799." At that instant she understood. *Do I dare?*

With quivering hands, she took the book from the shelf, found a spot at the end of the aisle, and leaned against the wall. She flipped through the book quickly until she found a section on herself and Louis. She skimmed the first page and read about her coming from Austria to Versailles. She turned a few pages and stopped abruptly when she saw a painting of an older woman with three small children surrounding an empty crib. *Oh my God!* The image resembled her, but it felt like she was staring into the face of someone else. There was extreme sadness in her eyes, and she wondered what had happened in her life to cause such unhappiness. *This is too much to take in!* But she could not stop. She continued turning page after page, not reading the print, just the section headings, too apprehensive of what she might find out. *Put the book down,* her spirit screamed, as her quivering hand slowly turned one more page. Her face went pale. Her world went dark. The book fell from her grasp and she slid slowly down the wall to the floor in a faint.

The section she had turned to was entitled, "*Marie Antoinette – Death by Guillotine.*"

Chapter 6

Marie's eyelids fluttered a moment before they opened, and she found herself staring into the eyes of two men bent over her. A small crowd had gathered around and slowly she realized she was still inside the bookshop in the belly of the Louvre. Trembling, too frightened to speak, she gave no response as they repeatedly asked her name. *How can I tell them my name?* They spoke in French and when she didn't respond, they tried English. She remained silent.

She listened intently as they discussed what to do with her. Feeling exposed, she gripped the neckline of her nightgown, realizing someone had unbuttoned her coat while she was unconscious. One of the men went through her bag mumbling something about identification. Within moments, two more men approached with a large bed on wheels and Marie was lifted onto it and strapped down. She fought against the restraints to no avail. They wheeled her out through the shop entrance and down the corridor toward the exit.

Wide-eyed, she scanned the hall, having no idea where they were taking her. She was no longer just a face in the crowd and it wouldn't be long until her identity would be discovered. *But why would anyone suspect I am Marie Antoinette who lived over*

200 years ago? It certainly didn't make sense to her, and most assuredly wouldn't make sense to anyone else. The book flashed in her mind. She had a sense she would not be well received if they realized who she was. *Will they try to kill me? Who are these men? I must get away!* Her body shook with fear.

The bed was wheeled through the crowd and out a side exit. The men stopped suddenly, and she felt the bed being lowered to the ground and then the men picked it up and shoved it headfirst into a compact space. One of the men remained with her, and the other closed and latched two swinging doors near her feet. Marie heard and felt a low rumble, and suddenly they were moving! A loud whining sound pierced her ears and she realized she was inside one of the moving objects she had been so frightened of. The speed at which it traveled made her head spin and bounced her around until she thought she would be sick to her stomach. Within minutes, the terrifying ordeal was over. The swinging doors opened and she was unloaded and wheeled into a large building and down a long hallway. She shielded her eyes from the bright light overhead. Finally, they turned the bed into a small room where she was unstrapped, her boots removed, and she was carefully placed onto another bed. All the men left except one, who lingered behind. He had a look of concern in his eyes. She eyed him suspiciously.

"Hello, I'm Ben. What's your name?" Despite Marie's emotional state she couldn't help but notice his appearance. He was thin, of medium height, with tanned skin, short black hair, and a slightly scruffy beard. She noticed his dark eyes as he spoke to her. "There's nothing to be afraid of. We are here to help you. Is there anyone I can call? We found no identification on you."

She shook her head no and turned away, wondering what he meant by "*call*" and "*identification.*"

Ben felt sorry for her. She was so small and frail. He tried again to get her to speak, but she remained silent. A few more seconds went by, and one of the other men came through the door. "We have another call," he said. "Let's go."

"Are you sure there's nothing I can do to help you?" She turned toward the wall, ignoring him, and he wondered aloud if she really understood. "A nurse will be in here shortly. I'm sure they'll take good care of you." Remaining silent, she turned her head slightly and watched as he picked up his bag and turned to leave.

Once Ben was gone, Marie knew she had to get out of there. Yesterday she was so desperate to find another human being, but now, being taken against her will, she felt completely vulnerable. Not ready to answer the questions she knew would come, she stood up and steadied herself on the side of the bed. Looking around for her bag, but not seeing it anywhere, she quickly pulled on her boots and silently opened the door. Looking left and right, she saw no one in sight, but heard voices around the corner. Tiptoeing across the hall and ducking into a doorway marked ESCALIERS, she went down the stairs and out the first door she came to, and found herself standing in an alley. Marie was back on the streets of Paris, only this time without food or money.

Her feet ached from all the walking from the train, and painful blisters had formed on both heels. The boots she wore were at least two sizes too big; her tiny feet swam in them. She traveled along the maze of streets aimlessly. All around her were people sitting outside cafés with friends, laughing, talking, and enjoying a meal together. She had never felt so alone in her entire life.

When she came to the Seine, she walked down a steep walkway to the shore. She found a secluded bench between two trees, sat down, and stared out over the water, contemplating her next move. As darkness fell, she noticed lights beginning to glow all around her. There were twinkle lights in the trees, and golden beams of light shooting up the sides of the buildings across the water. *How extraordinary!* She had noticed the lighting in the Louvre and in the hospital, but in the daytime, it hadn't had the same impact.

A barge silently floated down the river passing right in front of her. The entire boat glowed from within. A glass dome enclosed a room full of people sitting at elegant tables, complete with white tablecloths and crystal glasses. She found the entire scene enchanting.

Marie was transported back to Versailles and the grand dinners she was served every night—exquisite food, expertly prepared and presented in an artistic fashion. Nonetheless, she did not enjoy mealtime. It was court custom that many meals were eaten in full view of an audience. At first, she was quite self-conscious, never able to fully relax, always aware that every move she made as well as every word she said was seen and heard by strangers. Eyes and ears were everywhere, but after a while, she learned to ignore the onlookers.

In her reminiscence, her thoughts flooded back to what she had read in the bookshop. Biting her lower lip, she took a deep breath and refused to let her mind dwell on it. The story was too horrifying to think about, unfathomable. Within moments, from sheer exhaustion both mentally and physically, she stretched out on the bench and fell asleep.

* * *

It was difficult to sleep on the hard ground, especially tonight with the icy wind blowing across the river. As he shifted his body to try and get comfortable, his frustration grew. He didn't know how much longer he would be able to cope. An unseen force had altered his life completely and the confusion and desperation he felt was palpable.

He thought back to when it all started, just three days ago... Immediately and without warning, they were after him. His only choice was to get out, get out as fast as he could. Sprinting blindly, he ran out of the palace, across the front courtyard and into the street. He heard a loud screech just as he was hit from behind and his body catapulted forward. He rolled across the pavement, feeling excruciating pain in his left leg. Completely disoriented, he jumped up. Dragging his injured leg along the ground, he crossed over into a park across the way. Glancing back, he saw two men running toward him, and witnesses pointing and yelling in his direction.

Running through the park, and out the gate at the far end, he crouched behind a huge metal box in an alley behind a row of shops. Panting and shaking uncontrollably, he felt blood seeping through the leg of his trousers. The front of his white, lace shirt was ripped to shreds, and his overcoat was filthy. He adjusted his wig that haphazardly sat atop his head. He had no idea how he came to be here or why they were after him. He leaned back against the smelly container, stretched out his wounded leg, and passed out from the pain.

Chapter 7

A warm hand gently shook Marie's shoulder, and for a moment she thought it was one of her maids and she was back at Versailles. She opened her eyes slowly and into focus came a man. His soft voice was familiar; it was the man from the hospital.

"What are you doing here? Are you all right?" he asked. Marie remained silent as she quickly sat up on the bench and nervously smoothed her coat of its wrinkles. Ben waited, feeling a bit impatient with her refusal to talk to him. "What's wrong? Why won't you speak?"

Marie's heart pounded in her chest. Short of running away as she had from the hospital, she felt she had no choice. In the faintest whisper she spoke, "Sir, how... how did you locate me?"

"Finally! What are you doing here sleeping on a bench? Do you not have anywhere to stay the night?" Marie stared straight ahead. "Can I take you somewhere? Get you something to eat? I promise I won't hurt you."

Marie's mind raced as she quickly assessed her situation. She had no food, no money, and worse, no plan, but she couldn't let him know that. "No. I do not require your assistance. I am quite well."

Ben chuckled at her response. "You know, sleeping all night in the cold by the river does not seem like a good idea to me. Why don't you let me help you? I actually live very close to here."

Marie raised her regal shoulders as she took a deep breath. "Sir, let me assure you that I am perfectly capable of taking care of myself. Just leave me please." Her shoulders sagged.

"Fine, if that's what you want." Ben turned and went up the dark walkway. As he reached the street level, he turned back for one last look. She sat there, motionless, staring across the water. *She's crazy anyway, what do I care?* But he felt torn. He didn't feel right leaving her there, alone, in the cold. She had an air about her, but also an unmistakable vulnerability. He hesitated, and finally turned and began walking toward home.

Weary, Marie silently rose to her feet, glanced up and down the river, and then looked up the incline and saw Ben, just as he turned the corner and went out of sight. *Should I go with him? He doesn't seem to have any intention of harming me.* She was so tired of her indecision, her inability to think quickly and decisively. Unexpectedly, she saw movement among a stand of trees a few feet beyond the walkway Ben had just taken. A shadowy figure stepped out into the dim glow of the light post. Immediately she recognized him as the man in black, the man she had encountered twice before.

"Mademoiselle?" He took a step toward her as he spoke, and her instincts told her to run—*RUN NOW!*

She raced to the top of the walkway and called out to Ben. He immediately turned, and was shocked to see her running toward him. He stopped and waited, not sure what to expect.

"I decided... I decided I will allow you to accompany me to your residence."

"Allow me? Well, la-di-da."

Marie looked at him strangely. "Have you changed your mind sir?"

"No." Ben cocked his head. "I was only joking. And you don't have to call me sir." As they walked through the streets, he tried to make conversation, but again, she fell silent. She was different than any girl he had ever met. Her way of speaking was distinct, yet peculiar. Even her walk was different. As they made their way, she kept looking back. "Are you looking for someone?" She shook her head. He sensed she was afraid, but was doing everything she could to hide it.

Minutes later Ben stopped in front of a massive cream-colored building, pushed open a large red lacquer door, and held it open for her as she entered. She could not believe she was going with him, but continued following him along a cobblestone walkway that led through a quiet courtyard. They went through a second set of doors, which opened to a spiral staircase. Up, up, up they climbed to the fourth floor. Turning left, he stopped, fumbled for his keys, and within moments they were standing in a dark room.

Ben clicked on the light and Marie squinted from the sudden brightness. As her eyes adjusted, she was surprised and relieved to find quite a pleasant room. He tossed his keys into a porcelain bowl sitting on a small mahogany chest and hung his coat and scarf on a hook near the door. "Can I hang up your coat?" he asked. She shook her head no, remembering she only had her nightgown on underneath.

She stood by the door, taking in the rest of the room. To her immediate right was a small, open kitchen with gleaming metal furniture, and long counters of polished stone. The cabinets had glass doors that were lit from within where she could see cups, plates, glasses and bowls. To her left stood a tiny round dining table with 2 chairs. The wall beside the table was completely covered with a series of tall shelves, full of books, framed photos, and various objets d'art. Along the back wall were two full-length double glass doors covered in sheer shades and in between them stood an antique desk. In the corner was a white, ornate fireplace with a carved mantle over it, holding a few candles and a stack of books. In front of the fireplace was a small couch covered in dark-striped fabric, a down-filled upholstered chair of forest green corduroy and a matching footstool.

On the other side of the room were two doors and in between them stood a long, low 18th century chest of drawers. Over it hung an impressionist painting of a fishing village by the sea. The door to the right of the chest was slightly ajar and although it was dark, she sensed it was the bedroom.

Ben went about his business, seeming to understand that it might be a bit longer before Marie opened up to him. "I'll make us something to eat."

Her eyes followed him carefully as he walked over to the kitchen, filled a kettle with water and put it on the stove. He carefully cut up an apple and placed it on a plate along with a small triangle of Brie, then broke a baguette into four pieces. Placing the food on the table and pulling a chair out, he motioned for her to sit down.

The kettle on the stove began to whistle. Ben made two cups of chamomile tea and placed one before her. Marie relaxed a little, beginning to feel she could trust him. So far he had proven himself kind and generous, and besides, he was all she had between her and the confusing world just beyond the apartment walls. They ate in silence as she searched her mind for something to say. She drew a deep breath, tilted her head down and quietly spoke, "Thank you."

"I thought you might be hungry."

"Yes, I..." Her voice trailed off.

"Can you at least tell me your name?"

She hesitated. "It's... Marie."

"Where are you from?"

She paused, not sure what to say. Finally, she came out with it, "Versailles." She did not understand that he assumed she meant the town of Versailles, not the palace.

"Oh, I imagined you were from far away," Ben laughed. "Would you like me to call someone or arrange for you to catch the train home?"

"No."

"Why not?"

Not sure what to say, she remained still.

"Do you not have any money?" Ben waited. "Look, I'm only trying to help. But you have to talk to me so I—"

"Why must you ask so many questions?" she said with exasperation.

Ben held his hands up. "Okay, okay. I'm just trying to help."

"I allowed you to accompany me, isn't that enough?"

"What do you mean 'allowed' "?

"I... I'm sorry." Marie looked down, but couldn't think of anything else to say.

Without prying further, he imagined all sorts of reasons why she couldn't, or wouldn't, go back to where she came from. He hoped he would find out eventually. She was aloof, but he still felt compassion for her.

"Well, you're welcome to stay here tonight if you feel comfortable with that. You can sleep in my bedroom and I'll sleep in here on the couch. We can decide what to do tomorrow. How does that sound?"

"That will be acceptable." It was all Marie could manage to say, knowing she had no other option besides the cold, dark night just beyond the apartment doors.

Ben led her to the tiny bedroom. He opened the bottom drawer in his dresser and retrieved a pair of men's flannel pajamas. "These have never been worn. They were a Christmas gift from my sister." As he handed them to Marie, he stopped short. He hurried to the other room and returned with her bag. "I went back to check on you at the hospital. They said you had disappeared. I told them I knew you, so they gave me your bag. I know the watchman there too, and he allowed me to look at the security camera tapes and I saw which direction you took when you left. I brought your bag here, dropped it off and decided to search for you. That's when I found you sleeping by the Seine."

She didn't understand any of what he said regarding the security cameras but did not let on. She was relieved to have her bag back. She placed it on the floor by her feet. "Thank you very much."

Ben went into the bathroom and laid out a new toothbrush and some clean towels. "Is there anything else I can get you?"

"No." Marie felt a little embarrassed for being so rude. He was obviously a kind man. Her manners returned. "I am humbled by your kindness."

Ben shrugged and showed her to the tiny bathroom and quietly closed the door. The water at the sink and toilet did not work automatically as the ones had at Versailles and looked slightly different from the ones in the Louvre. She considered asking Ben for help, but decided against it. After trial and error, she figured it out and managed to wash her face. She read the back of the toothpaste tube and the toothbrush package and tried to clean her teeth. The toothpaste burned her mouth and she spit it out immediately.

Marie had noticed when she was in the Louvre and on the streets, that cleanliness of the body was different from her time. She decided to take a bath, as she hadn't had one in days. She noticed a bottle of shampoo by the tub and after reading the label, she took a quick bath and washed her hair. It had to be quick, the water was leaving the tub as quickly as it came in. It felt strange to have to do so much for herself. Even as a child, a princess in Vienna, she had had servants around her. As dauphine it was worse. All her personal grooming was done for her. It was one of the most hated parts of her life at Versailles. No matter how much she protested, it was pressed upon her. Still trying to find her way among those at court, she had little choice but to carry on as told. She found herself acting the same way with Ben. How she wished she could just come out with it: the entire story.

She found a comb in one of the drawers, and combed her hair out carefully. She put the rosary back around her neck, put on the pajamas, and slowly opened the door to return to the bedroom. Ben's back was to her as he washed the dishes. He had left the bedroom door slightly ajar, pulled back the covers, and turned a tiny lamp on next to the bed. She was embarrassed to be seen in the pajamas so she softly closed the bedroom door behind her. The lamp remained on all night. She had no idea how to turn it off.

Chapter 8

Ben heard the bedroom door close quietly. He finished washing the dishes and placed them back into the cupboard. He was always a tidy person, making sure everything was back in its proper place before going to bed. But everything wasn't in its proper place tonight. He would not be sleeping in his bed, instead a complete stranger would be, albeit a beautiful stranger. He considered his actions puzzling, completely out of character, but there was something about this woman he couldn't walk away from.

Ben had come across many interesting people during his time working as a paramedic, but no one like Marie. He thought back to the training he completed a year ago. One of the first things he learned was to not get involved with his patients on a personal level. He was to take care of their immediate health needs, and if needed, get them to the hospital as quickly as possible. It had all been so simple, until now.

Walking over to the tiny closet in the corner of the living room, he took out an old quilt his grandmother had made, and a small pillow. He kept these things stowed away for when his sister Diana came to visit from London. They were quite close and enjoyed spending time together. He always gave his sister the use of his bedroom, so another night spent on the couch wouldn't bother him a bit. His father had taught him to treat women with the utmost respect and deference.

The women Ben met since coming to live in Paris all seemed reserved and unapproachable. Even though he had grown up around French women his whole life, he had yet to figure them out. They rarely showed vulnerability. That's one reason he found Marie so interesting. For the first time ever, he felt he had met a woman that needed him, and needed him badly. He just couldn't figure out why.

Ben lay in the dark for over an hour, restless. He couldn't get to sleep, having so many questions in his mind. *Why doesn't she open up? What is she afraid of? Why did she pass out in the bookstore? If she's sick, why did she leave the hospital so abruptly without so much as a word to anyone? And most importantly, why did I find her sleeping on a cold, lonely bench along the Seine? So many questions...* He finally fell asleep thinking of the lost, lonely woman that slept in his bed, right in the very next room.

Chapter 9

Light spilled in from the large windows of the bedroom, and Marie awoke feeling better than she had since her ordeal began. She heard sounds coming from the other room and realized Ben was already up. The smell of food drove her from the bed. He smiled broadly when she came into the room. "Good morning. I hope you slept well."

"I did."

He waited for her to respond further, and when she did not, he nodded for her to sit down at the dining table. Within moments, a steaming cup of black coffee was placed before her, as well as a small glass of orange juice. Feeling a draft, she noticed the large French doors of the apartment were ajar. Outside was a lovely balcony, complete with a blue metal table and 2 chairs. Large stone pots on each end contained tall ornamental bushes.

"May I step outside?"

"Of course. Take your coffee, it's chilly out there. I'll bring you some bread and jam in a moment."

"Oh... uhh... I'll remain here." Marie was not used to such casual dining, and was not comfortable eating outside or carrying her cup around. Mealtime was formal in her life, every day of the year.

A newspaper was lying open on the table, and when she glanced at the date, her heart skipped a beat. There it was again in black and white, reality. *How can it be the twenty-first century? Will I ever return?* She added some sugar to her coffee and twirled her spoon round and round the cup aimlessly. Her mind drifted back to the incredible 18th birthday party that was given in her in honor just over a week ago. No expense was spared. The Venus Drawing Room, Marie's favorite area in Versailles, was decorated in grand style. Long tables were set and laden with silver candlesticks and filigree baskets full of breads and pastries. Trays and trays were brought in with pyramids of fresh fruits, flowers, and other delectable foods. There were buckets of Champagne and of course presents, lots of presents. An orchestra played continuously and she encouraged everyone to dance. It was a perfect night, one in which she had enjoyed court life, even if just for an evening. How odd that her previous life now seemed a million miles away. Lost in thought, she didn't notice the croissant that had been placed on the table in front of her. She was startled back to the present when Ben sat down. He was ready to confront her, especially since he had noticed her nightgown hanging in the bathroom. He wanted to know why this young woman was walking around Paris in her nightgown.

"So, I'm ready to hear your story. What's going on with you?"

Marie tried to collect her thoughts.

"Well?"

"My... my present situation... is exceedingly difficult to describe. I... would rather not speak of it."

"Rather not speak of it? What do you mean?" Ben waited. "You're going to have to talk sooner or later. You had nowhere to sleep last night. Are you homeless?"

"What do you mean?"

"I mean, do you have a home?"

"I told you, I... I'm from Versailles."

"Can I take you there?"

"No. I cannot return to my previous residence."

"Why not? Did someone hurt you? Are you in danger?"

"No."

Ben was getting frustrated with her noncommittal attitude. "Just come out with it. I took you in last night. I think I'm owed some sort of explanation and I'm tired of waiting around for you to explain."

Marie was not used to being challenged. "How dare you address me that way! You have no authority to demand anything of me."

"Who exactly do you think you are?"

"You have no idea to whom you are speaking!"

"No, I don't, and I'm beginning not to care either." Annoyed, he took his plate over to the counter and continued eating with his back to her. It occurred to him that she might be a criminal running from the law or something like that. Whatever it was, he was no longer sure he wanted to be mixed up in it. He noticed once again, her way of speaking was archaic, as if she were speaking a part in a period film. *Maybe she's crazy.*

Marie was stunned. Not only had her attitude taken a swing, but his as well. She had to remain calm and focus on how she might tell him the truth. She must remember she was not in her century, and in fact, not the dauphine any longer.

They finished their meal in silence. Ben tidied up with Marie eyeing him as he worked. He wasn't a servant, and in her experience, men simply didn't cook and clean the way he did unless they were in someone's charge. She was quite accustomed to being served, but now with them at odds, she felt ill at ease.

It was Ben's day off from the hospital so his initial plan was to take her wherever she wanted to go. Now, it seemed hopeless. She was unwilling to tell him anything about herself, and despite her arrogant attitude he felt sorry for her. He knew she was hiding something and he chose to wait her out.

"Look, I'm off work today. What would you like to do?"

"I'm... not sure."

"I'm guessing you don't have any family or friends here in Paris."

"Well... no." Marie shifted nervously in her chair. "I would like to procure a few items of clothing. I really don't have any with me."

"Okay. If you'd like, you can borrow some of my clothes and we can go out shopping. You certainly can't go out in my pajamas, or in the nightgown hanging in the bathroom."

She looked down and realized she had forgotten how she was dressed. She had pulled the drawstring pajama pants as tightly as she could, but even so, had to hold them up as she walked. Following him into his bedroom, she noticed his size, and although he wasn't a large man, he was certainly bigger and taller than she. He pulled out a pair of dark jeans, a striped black and white starched shirt, and a pair of black socks. "This will have to do for now. I know of a store not far from here. I'm sure you can find a few things there."

Ben left the room, quietly closing the door behind him. Marie pulled on the jeans. They were too long, and the waist stood out from her petite frame. She tucked the shirt in, pushed up the sleeves, and rolled up the bottom of the pants, then put on the socks and her boots. Turning to the mirror, she was horrified. *I can't be seen like this!* Hurriedly removing the ill-fitting clothes, she retrieved her nightgown from the bathroom and put it on along with her coat. She had walked the streets like this before, so today would be no different.

Marie walked out. "Thank you, but I will continue wearing my own clothes." As they got ready to leave, Marie took the money out of her bag and gave it to Ben. "It's all I have." *All she has?* He glanced down and quickly counted out 300 euros. He placed the money in his pocket, wondering why she felt it necessary to hand it over to him.

Together they exited the building and walked along the sidewalk, dodging others as they went. This time of the morning the streets were always busy. He led Marie to the Metro stop around the corner. She grabbed his hand tightly as they descended the stairs to the station underground, fearful she would lose him in the crowd. He stopped at a window, bought her a ticket and she went through the turnstile. Then he waved his pass-card over the magic eye and proceeded through behind her. They waited just moments on the platform, and as the metro sped toward them, she jumped back with a start. He looked back at her.

"It's really crowded today. Stay with me, and don't let go of my hand," Ben said. Marie simply nodded and did as she was told.

Chapter 10

Ben took Marie to a popular clothing store on the Boulevard de la Madeleine. She followed closely behind him, eyes wide at the sheer expanse of the store. Once they entered the women's department Ben paused in the aisle and waited. Her confusion was apparent. Seeing other women going through the racks, she cautiously moved forward and looked at the rack closest to her. "I hardly think anything in this section will fit you," Ben said. She stopped and glanced over at another rack, then back to him. He nodded. She took that to mean she was on the right track, all the while trying to appear knowledgeable, but failing.

She was accustomed to fabrics being brought to the palace for her to select from, and she loved taking part in the overall design and details of each dress, as well as the design of the undergarments. The clothes were then expertly tailored to fit her tiny frame and brought back to her for final approval. Her style was copied all over the country and beyond, even at her young age. Now she roamed around like a lost child. Finally, Ben walked over and assisted her in choosing a few dresses. "Would you like to try them on?"

"Here?"

"Of course, here. You can even wear one out if you like." Ben was puzzled by her behavior. She was so childlike. He didn't believe she had any mental issues, but he could not put his finger on what issue she obviously had. She had limited understanding of normal life. Her mystery deepened.

Ben directed her over to the dressing rooms and she timidly entered a stall and closed the door. She examined the clothes, finding them lacking in design and construction. She pulled one of the dresses over her head and looked in the mirror. It was a simple long sleeved cream-colored knit dress with black buttons down the back and a wide black patent leather belt to cinch in the waist. She was certainly used to cinching in her waist, but the rest of the outfit left her feeling exposed in an uncomfortable way. Modern clothes were simple in construction and although comfortable compared to what she normally wore, she didn't know if she would ever get used to the looseness, the free feeling they had on her body.

Finally, Marie came out and handed Ben three dresses she thought would work. They wandered over to the lingerie section and suddenly they both felt self-conscience. Ben excused himself and wandered over toward the shoes, leaving Marie alone. A salesclerk noticed her, walked over and said, "May I help you find something?"

"Yes, please, but I'm not really sure what I need."

"Is this your first time here?"

"Yes, it is." Marie blushed.

The saleswoman assumed she was a young teen, and this was the first time she was purchasing undergarments on her own. The woman quickly took Marie under her wing and guided her to the items she needed. When finished, Marie wandered over to the shoe area where Ben waited.

This part wasn't easy either. Marie's feet were extremely narrow and there were very few shoes that fit. Finally, she chose a pair of quilted black ballet flats, along with some tights to go with them.

Once Ben paid for the items, he instructed the clerk to remove the tags from the clothing indicating that Marie wished to change into them before they left the store. She returned to the dressing room and took quite some time getting dressed. Glancing at herself in the mirror, she was glad to not have to continue wearing her nightgown and oversized boots any longer.

Beautiful sunshine and mild temperatures greeted them outside. Ben decided they would walk to Place de la Concorde, and cross over to a small café he frequented when in the area.

Marie was content to follow along, carrying some of the smaller packages. They crossed the busy intersection and walked toward the open square, pausing to enjoy the ornate fountains. Marie found them quite familiar, similar in design to those at Versailles. She couldn't help but laugh as the spray from the fountains caused them to quickly retreat to a safe distance. In between the fountains was a tall, graceful stone structure topped with a gold pyramid that reached toward the sky. As Marie looked up, she fell backwards, Ben turning just in time to catch her. Although embarrassed, Marie smiled. She was beginning to let go, ever so slightly and enjoy herself.

They were halfway around the square, when Marie paused and looked at the ground. Her pale skin turned translucent, as she stood there, frozen. Ben's eyes followed hers, and there embedded between the cobblestones was a small brass plaque. On the plaque the following words were engraved...

THIS PLACE
INAUGURATED IN 1763
ORIGINALLY CALLED
PLACE OF LOUIS XV FROM NOVEMBER 1792 TO MAY 1795
THEN RENAMED PLACE OF THE REVOLUTION
WAS THE MAIN PLACE FOR PUBLIC EXECUTIONS
INCLUDING THAT OF
LOUIS XVI, JANUARY 21, 1793
AND OF
MARIE ANTOINETTE, OCTOBER 16, 1793.

He looked up. Marie was breathing in and out so quickly he was afraid she would hyperventilate, so he led her away from the plaque. She leaned into him as they walked.

Ben's mind whirled. *Why is she disturbed by the plaque... something that happened so many years ago?* By the time they crossed the busy intersection at the opposite end of the square, he noticed tears streaming down her cheeks. *That's it,* he thought. He was going to demand answers from her. He felt it was imperative to her mental health, and their growing friendship. He wasn't yet ready to admit to himself that his feelings for her were growing, despite her perplexing behavior.

Chapter 11

Ben led Marie into a quiet café and chose a table in the back corner. Once they sat down, Ben immediately tried to pin her down. "Look, you've got to tell me what's going on. Who exactly are you? What is your story?"

Marie knew she could no longer hide her identity from Ben. The more time she spent with him, the more she trusted him. He had been patient and understanding with her and she longed to tell him the truth—the entire confusing, unbelievable truth. Marie proceeded cautiously, carefully weighing each of her words, watching for Ben's reaction.

"Well... my birthplace is Austria, but I reside at Versailles. Actually, I've lived at Versailles since I was fourteen." She regarded him carefully, but he gave no reaction. Marie continued, holding her head high as she spoke. "My name is Marie... Marie Antoinette." Her heart pounded in anticipation.

"Wow, your parents must have had some sense of humor." Ben rolled his eyes.

"Whatever do you mean?"

"Seriously, what is your real name?"

"At birth, my name was Maria Antonia Josepha Johanna, Archduchess of Austria. Now it's Marie Antoinette, Dauphine of France."

"Come on, first you tell me nothing, and now this. If you'll be honest with me, maybe I can help you." As the words came out of his mouth, the look on her face was telling. He realized she might actually mean *the* Marie Antoinette. His mind flashed back to the book he saw beside her on the floor of the bookstore, as well as the plaque in the square, both having a connection to the historical Marie Antoinette. *This woman delusional, but her manner is completely serious. If she's mentally unstable, I must be gentle.* He decided to play along and see exactly how far she would take it. *Maybe*, he hoped, *she just has an odd sense of humor.*

"Are you saying you are *the* Marie Antoinette, the former queen of France?"

"No, I'm not the queen, I'm the dauphine."

"How do you explain being here, now, in this century?"

Her words tumbled out. "I can't explain it. I woke up two days ago in my bed at Versailles. The palace was empty, completely abandoned. I stayed the night, and when I awoke the next morning I heard voices. My situation was unknown to me, but I had seen a calendar and I was frightened. I quickly slipped out of the palace and walked through the town unnoticed. I took the train here, to Paris." She paused and then continued, "I know this is hard to believe, and I find it hard to believe myself, but this feels real. I'm still me, but I have no idea how I got here." Her eyes looked deep into his for the first time since they met, silently begging him to believe her.

Ben looked away, wondering what to say next. *She obviously needs professional help.* He turned and looked at her, noticing how her porcelain skin and white-blonde hair enhanced her aquamarine eyes. Last night and this morning she seemed fragile, vulnerable, but at this moment she was a whisper of a woman, almost an apparition. *Is it my imagination?* Ben shook his head abruptly to come out of the spell. He knew he had to keep his cool so he could help her, rather than be taken in by her delusions and her beautiful face.

"Is that why you fainted in the bookstore and nearly passed out in the square... because of what you read about Marie Antoinette?"

"Yes... can you tell me, is it true? Is that what happens to her—to me? I'm... beheaded?"

"Well... Marie Antoinette was beheaded... I believe in 1793."

"Can you tell me why?"

Ben sat there quietly. How would he sum up years of history to the woman before him, who actually thought she was a part of it?

"There were a lot of events that led up to it. Actually, the story is perhaps the most pivotal moment in all of French history, known throughout the world."

Marie sat back in her chair, dumbfounded. At that moment, the waiter interrupted their conversation. Ben ordered onion soup and red wine for them both. As soon as the waiter walked away, Marie leaned forward and spoke ever so softly, "It's impossible that I, an 18-year-old childless dauphine of France, could possibly play that big of a role in history."

"But she did, and at the time of her death, she was the queen. As far as children go, I believe there were four of them."

"That's simply impossible," she mumbled.

"Why do you say that?"

"Well… it just is."

"Why?"

"It's difficult to explain the reasons, but Louis and I have been married for years, and we have yet… to consummate the marriage." Ben vaguely remembered reading something about that, but chose to let the subject go, for now.

Their soup was delivered to the table and the two of them ate quietly. Marie's mind whirled. She was surprised she had an appetite at all. They sat in silence lost in their own thoughts, and then Marie had an idea.

"It's obvious you don't believe I am who I say I am, and honestly I don't blame you. But I was wondering if you have a French history book back at the apartment? I would like to examine it and see for myself exactly what has happened."

"I think I still have a book from a class I took at university. It will have the history of Marie Antoinette and the revolution."

"Revolution?"

Ben ignored her question, paid the bill, and they stepped outside into the afternoon sun. Marie shielded her eyes with her hand. It seemed strange to have the sun shining so brightly when her world—her very existence—was confusing and dim.

They rode the metro back to his neighborhood with very little conversation. When they entered the apartment half an hour later, Ben turned to her. "Marie, I want you to know, you can stay here with me as long as you want. I want to help you sort out this mystery—to figure out who you really are and where you come from."

"Thank you so much, that's very kind of you." She took a deep breath, "But you must understand... I know exactly who I am, and once I learn how I got here, I will find a way to return."

Chapter 12

The clock ticked slowly. Darkness fell. The only sound in the apartment was the flutter of paper, the pages from a well-worn book that had sat on the shelf, long forgotten.

As Marie read, she certainly didn't feel like the main character in the book and yet, for chapters and chapters, she was the central figure. It was a tragedy, hard to comprehend. She barely recognized herself. She read about the lovely times she had had: her incredible wardrobe, hairstyles, and how she was the trendsetter of her time. Her personal sex life with Louis was blazoned across the pages in such detail that it made her blush. She read of things that she had no idea were going on right under her nose at Versailles. She read the account of Louis' grandfather's tragic death from smallpox, and of her and Louis' ascension to the throne. She also learned about the children she had had and how she had lost two of them. She wondered how she and Louis had finally managed to conceive.

There was a lot of detail in the book, some of which she found preposterous. Details were given, although the author admitted it was rumor, of the story of Count Axel de Fersen from Sweden, her supposed lover. She couldn't imagine such a thing. She had met Axel briefly just last week at her birthday party. Although Louis had problems in the bedroom, and she remained a virgin, they had grown quite close. Their affection for one another had deepened, especially during the last year. She couldn't imagine having an affair under any circumstances. But after reading the account of her arrest and imprisonment and almost escape, aided by Axel, she wondered... maybe there was a relationship between her and this stranger. She marveled at how much she had changed in the course of those years, and at her utter lack of personal responsibility, as well her extravagant spending and gambling once she became queen.

When she got to the chapter about her and Louis' death, she chose to stop there. No use reading any further. She knew the eventual outcome, and the fear of reading the actual account kept her from going on. She skipped the gory details, and in the end, was relieved to read that her daughter had made it back to Austria and lived a long, full life.

She closed the book, shut her eyes, and leaned back into the sofa, so many thoughts whirling in her head. There were missed opportunities she and Louis had had to change the future, but they didn't see it. They had had such an undying devotion to the monarchy and to their duty that they stuck with it until their deaths, thinking it was the right thing to do.

Marie found it fascinating how much she had changed during her years in prison, maturing into a thoughtful, brave, mature young woman. She had had such courage and yet, Louis had been unable to accept the reality of their situation. Incapable of leading, he had withdrawn into his shell. As she considered all the events, she felt detached, finding it hard to accept.

Her head hurt, her heart ached, and she was utterly exhausted from the tension. She jumped when something suddenly moved across the room. It was Ben. *Ben...* she had totally forgotten where she was. He was sitting at his desk with his back to her. He sensed her movement and turned around.

"So, you've finished reading?"

"Yes."

"Are you all right?"

"I think so. It's hard to imagine. It's confusing, and a lot of it is very hurtful. I'm actually embarrassed that you know all this about me. I feel very exposed, even of a life I have not yet lived." She felt the color rise in her cheeks.

"Don't be. French people do not speak of the revolution often, but it's a part of the fabric of our culture that is always present just under the surface." Ben studied her expression as he spoke the next words. "Look, I know who you think you are, but we both know it isn't possible. Can you tell me anything else you remember about the past two days?"

"I've told you everything. Louis and I retired to bed as usual. It was the year 1773. When I awoke the next morning, I was alone. There wasn't a soul at Versailles. I searched the entire palace and the grounds and found no one. I spent another night in my room, having nowhere to go, and having no understanding of what was happening. When I awoke the next morning, Versailles was teaming with strange people, so I fled."

Ben furrowed his brow, "Versailles is closed on Mondays, so that explains why no one was there the first day. The people you saw the next day are workers and tourists. People come from all over the world to visit the palace. It's quite famous, as you can imagine. People have always been interested in how royalty lived. There is very little royalty left in the world, so it's fascinating to many."

"Very little royalty left?"

"Yes. Most of the ones that remain are powerless figureheads."

"What about France?"

"No, there is no royal family anymore."

"Are you saying when Louis and I died, that was the end of the monarchy?"

"Basically, yes."

"I cannot imagine..." She stared into space. "Well, Versailles has certainly changed. I mean, the shell of it is the same, but the grandness is gone. So many of the paintings, the furniture, all the special things are no more. All my personal possessions are gone. According to the book, most of the treasures were stolen or destroyed during the worst of the... what did they call it... the revolution?"

"Yes, well, it's surprising Versailles is still standing at all," Ben said quietly.

Heaviness hung in the air. Marie knew that Ben did not believe for one moment that she was actually Marie Antoinette from the 18th century, and she didn't blame him. What bothered her was that he was such a kind person. She felt safe and comfortable in his presence, and desperately wanted his acceptance and trust. He didn't seem to want anything from her. Most of the people that had befriended her at Versailles wanted favors or help in some way, usually looking for titles or appointments that would give them status in life. There was a specific hierarchy in her time, that didn't seem to exist in this century. She was quite used to having everything done for her, everything taken care of in her life, without her having to give it much thought. Now, she was in control of her life and could make her own decisions. She felt confused by her situation, but empowered as well, knowing she was on her own, and yet... she needed Ben desperately.

"I understand it is difficult for you to accept who I am, and I do not expect you to, not yet."

"Okay..."

"Is the offer still good for me to continue residing with you, at least until I sort things out?"

"Yes. I would like that very much."

It was late, and they were both tired. Once again, Marie retired to Ben's room and he spent another night on the couch. As he drifted off to sleep, he wondered what tomorrow would bring. Whatever happened, he knew he wanted to get closer to her, understand her, and help her.

Chapter 13

Marie awoke refreshed the next morning. The night before last she had slept from pure mental and physical exhaustion. Last night she had been able to sleep soundly, having shared her story with Ben. Even though he didn't believe her, she felt safe and secure for the first time since her ordeal began. Glancing at the clock on the bedside table she was surprised to see that it was past nine. She hadn't heard a sound from Ben, which suddenly made her uneasy. She quickly dressed and emerged from the bedroom.

The apartment was empty. Feeling a wave of panic, she looked around and noticed the dining table set for one. At her place was a croissant, and next to her plate, a folded piece of paper. The coffee was ready, so she poured herself a cup and sat down to read the contents of the note. She smiled. It was from Ben, of course. He wrote that he had to work a six-hour shift, and he should be back by noon. He told her to help herself to anything she wanted in the apartment. *An entire morning to myself! What a luxury!* She ate her breakfast quickly and looked around. *What shall I do?*

Deciding to take a long hot bath, she relished in her privacy. No one was there to draw the bath, or undress her. Through trial and error she figured out how to fill the tub with water. It felt strange, yet liberating to do things as she wished, when she wished. She relaxed in the tub, deciding to embrace her new life, if only for today. She wanted to experience life like a commoner—a commoner of this century. The women she had seen on the street seemed to come and go as they pleased. They possessed a confidence—a confidence she certainly didn't have, even with her royal title.

When the water cooled down to an uncomfortable temperature she finally got out of the tub, dressed, and tried to do something with her hair, which seemed hopeless. She had no choice but to wear it long and straight, but she did change her part to the side, thinking it was a bit more becoming.

Marie wandered back into the living area of the apartment and paced the room. Being alone was nice, but it was foreign to her, unsettling. Lingering in front of the bookcase filled with old and new books, she decided to read until Ben got home. She scanned the shelf and settled on an intriguing title, "*Da Vinci Code*" because she recognized the Mona Lisa on the cover and the name of the famous painter in the title. Settling on the couch, she grabbed the soft quilt folded on the corner and began reading. The story was confusing and the reading slow going. She could certainly read French, but it was not her first language, and the grammar in this book was quite different than what she was used to. She had noticed the same thing about Ben's speech and found many of his words unfamiliar.

After a while, she abandoned the book. Her eyes settled on a large, black, glass object sitting upright on the chest. She had no idea what it was. She studied the front of the box and remembered exploring the brass box full of money back at Versailles. Taking a deep breath, she cautiously pressed one of the buttons on the bottom edge and suddenly the box lit up. She screamed and fell backwards when a man appeared on the screen and began speaking to her. She scrambled, crouching behind the couch, hoping he hadn't seen her. She remained completely still, afraid to move while the man continued talking. What he was talking about she did not know and for the life of her, she couldn't figure out how the man got in the box, and soon she realized he wasn't addressing her at all.

She peeked around the corner of the couch, bravely stood up, then walked over and sat on the edge of the coffee table, dumbfounded. It was shocking when other people of all sorts came onto the screen, as well as buildings, furniture, food, and many other objects. She realized they couldn't all be in the box, and finally relaxed when it seemed they couldn't see her. Marie even tried speaking to the box, but no one responded, so she settled on the couch and watched the screen intently, finding the stories confusing and fascinating, and the sheer pace of the images bewildering. She marveled at all she saw, and when she heard Ben's key in the lock, she was shocked at how much time had passed.

"Hello. How are you?" said Ben.

"I'm well, thank you."

"Did you find something interesting to watch on TV?"

"TV? Is that what you call it?"

"Are you kidding me?" She shrugged and looked down embarrassed, although she had no reason to feel embarrassed. Ben realized she was still acting as the former Marie Antoinette. He wondered how long his patience would last. "Have you had it on the same channel this whole time?" he finally asked, noticing the remote was still on the shelf under the TV.

"I do not understand." Marie felt awkward, like a child that was caught doing something wrong. Ben sighed, and hung up his uniform coat on a hook by the door, and placed his medical bag on the floor under it.

"It's a little chilly in here. Do you want me to turn on the heat?"

"Turn ON the heat? What does that mean?" Ben looked at her a little exasperated. She decided to change the subject "No, I'm fine. Thank you for the breakfast you left for me. It was very kind of you."

"I didn't want to wake you this morning. I saw no need to. I work six-hour shifts, five days a week. I would like to work more hours, but that's all the government allows me right now. What have you been up to this morning, besides watching TV?"

"Well... I took a bath and started reading a book, but I found it confusing and difficult. I noticed the box... I mean... TV. I'm afraid I got a little lost in it."

"Yea, that happens. It's mindless entertainment."

Marie was not sure what he meant by that.

For the rest of the afternoon, they stayed in the apartment. She began to feel more at ease, despite some of the difficulties understanding her surroundings. She wasn't anxious to get back out into the confusing world outside. They discussed many things, but mainly, the subject was Ben. Marie was curious now that she was more relaxed and not as focused on her own survival.

She slowly dropped her usual defense, wanting to learn more about this man, her savior.

"Ben, you know almost everything about me, and I know nothing at all about you. Tell me about yourself."

"There's not a whole lot to tell. I was born in a small fishing village in the south of France. My mother and father met there. She was French, and my father is American. I have one sister, Diana. She's six years younger than me."

"How old are you?"

"Twenty-seven, and you?"

"I just turned 18."

"I thought you were young, but I didn't realize how young."

"Oh, but do continue, we are speaking of you now, not me."

"Okay, my parents met when my father was traveling. He's a travel writer, and was doing a story on coastal villages in France. He met my mother quite by accident, in a café I believe. My father left behind everything he had in America, and married her within a few weeks. They were very much in love, but both their families were against the marriage. It took a while, but by the time I was born, everyone had accepted one other. We were all one big happy family. I don't see my American grandparents often. They come to visit every few years. My sister and I have only been to see them once."

"Where do they live?"

"In Massachusetts on the eastern seaboard. Their house has a beautiful view of the Atlantic Ocean."

"Are you speaking of the British Colony?"

"Uhm... well, yes, although America is no longer controlled by the British."

"I see. What is your sister like?" Marie asked.

"She's full of life, always ready for an adventure. She was born when I was six. That's when we lost our mother. She died shortly after childbirth of an infection. It overtook her body in a few days, and there was nothing they could do to save her." He paused, lost in thought. Marie could tell he loved his mother, and the memory of her death seemed fresh.

"Mom was quite beautiful, and very spontaneous. Dad was more quiet and reserved. My sister is more like our mom, and I'm more like Dad. Once mom died, her parents took a large role in raising us. We stayed at their house a lot. It was in the same village. Dad continued to travel for his job, but when he was home, he took good care of us. My sister and I are close. I've always felt protective of her. My father instilled that in me. I've actually had a really good life, considering. Everyone in our village knew us, and helped keep an eye on us. We were a curiosity at times, being half-American, but they accepted us fully. Of course, I feel completely French, but my father made sure we understood American ways."

Marie listened intently to everything Ben said, simultaneously trying to sort out the meaning of many unfamiliar phrases he used. Slowly, her opinion of him changed. She realized she wasn't the only one that had experienced difficulties in life and she began to see Ben as a real person. For the past few days, she had thought of him merely as a provider of sorts, her lifeline. Oh, she liked him fine, but now she felt a tremendous compassion for him. She was accustomed to being waited on, provided for, and taken care of, but it was always out of someone else's sense of duty—their employment. Ben was helping her selflessly, with nothing to gain. The reality of this sunk in as she pictured the difficulties he had had in his life.

"How did you end up in Paris?" Marie asked, as they continued talking into the afternoon. It was getting chilly, and Ben busied himself building a fire.

"I came here to attend school. I was going to follow in my father's footsteps and become a writer. After a while, I realized it wasn't for me. I had always thought about the medical profession in the back of my mind, because of my mother's death. I wanted to help others, so I attended the Rescue Institute here in Paris, got a job with the hospital, and have been with the Urgent Medical Aid Service for over a year now."

"So you help the sick?"

"Yes, that's part of what I do."

"Do you like your work?"

"Yes, very much. Our training is rigorous, quite difficult in fact, much more so than in other countries. I've learned so much. I feel good when I'm helping people, making a difference, you know?"

No, Marie didn't know. She thought about her life, and how she didn't feel she contributed anything. It got even worse as she thought about her future. She knew she had been self-centered and self-serving. This behavior would end up costing her her very life, and those of her children. She suddenly felt overwhelmed with sadness and regret. Now she was stuck here, in the future. If only she could go back and return to her life with this fresh perspective, make better choices, and maybe even make a difference—not just in hairstyles and fashion, but a real difference—to other people less fortunate than her. Her feelings overcame her and she rushed into the bedroom and closed the door. She didn't want Ben to see her like this. She was still self-conscious around him, and embarrassed as she thought about her way of life. She felt he was thinking the same thing about her. She had never felt any remorse for the way she lived... she knew no other way. Now she was seeing her life though a different lens, the long reaching lens of history. She was also seeing the sheer contrast of the kind of life the man in the next room lived compared to her own.

A few minutes went by as she stood in the room, trying to get a hold of herself. She was facing the wall when Ben softly opened the door and walked up behind her. He wasn't sure what he had said to upset her. He carefully put his hand on her shoulder and whispered her name. She was overcome. She turned and buried her face in his chest and cried pent-up tears. He didn't say anything, or ask for an explanation. He instead stood quietly with her, stroking her hair, as she let free her emotions.

Chapter 14

Once Marie settled down, Ben pulled his shirttail out, dried her tears and they sat down on the side of the bed. "I'm ashamed of how I've lived my life so far. I mean, I never really thought about it until now. I've always obeyed, first my parents, and then later I obeyed the rules at court. I was raised to be polite, gracious, and agreeable. I always tried to please others, to make my mother proud. When I first arrived at Versailles, I was loved, celebrated by the people. But as time went by, it seemed no matter what I did, or how hard I tried, I was never really accepted. So instead of trying to better myself, I got bored. I spent outrageous sums of money on clothes, shoes, and jewelry. And as I have just read, it gets much worse. The waste was not only of the money, but also of my time, especially considering how quickly my life ends. Everything has been chosen for me, but still, I see opportunities I've missed to make my part of the world a better place." Marie closed her eyes and leaned into his chest, "Will I ever go back to my life in Versailles? What will happen if I do? What will happen if I don't?"

For the first time, Ben began to seriously consider the possibility that she was truly from the past. *How can she speak so passionately about her life, if it wasn't actually her life?* It suddenly seemed possible.

He looked down at her with fresh eyes. Most of the paintings he had seen of Marie Antoinette were from her older years as queen. Her hair was usually done up very fancy, piled high on the top of her head. The dresses she wore were big and voluminous. But here stood this woman, a mere wisp of a girl, dressed in modern clothing with her hair down, long and straight, but yes... her hair was the same white-blonde color from the paintings. Slowly Ben took her chin in his hand and raised her face to look at him. As he studied her, it was clear. She looked astonishingly like the woman in the paintings. He felt strange, suddenly cold and clammy. It was too much. He didn't understand these new feelings, but he felt a change come over him. He suddenly wanted to believe her! All at once it occurred to him that he could be holding the future queen of France in his arms. But no... not the future queen... the past queen?

He shook his head back and forth, as if to rearrange his thoughts, not believing he had almost bought into her world. He released her and abruptly left the room. He felt he had to get away, leave the apartment for a moment to collect his thoughts. He grabbed his jacket and scarf and called out, "I have to go out. I won't be long."

Marie stood by the bed, shocked. *Why is he leaving? Should I follow after him?* She took a few steps toward the door and paused. *No, I'll wait. I must trust that he'll be back.*

Ben walked the streets of his neighborhood, Le Marais. He passed by many of the trendy bars and cafés as he walked, not certain where he was going. He had to think, to clear his head.

Did he want to believe her, because he knew he was falling for her? Being from another time period was better than her being mentally ill, right? Ben laughed at his two choices. How could he possibly accept such a premise? He did not believe in aliens, or time travel. He was a reasonable person, but this situation was anything but reasonable.

He continued walking, mindlessly turning from Rue de Rivoli down another street and finally standing on a bridge overlooking the Seine. He stared out over the water, watching the moonlight dance over the ripples. His mind relaxed, letting thoughts come and go at will, taking time to slowly go over the events of the past few days. He finally decided to move on when he realized what bridge he was standing on: Pont Marie. Reminders of her were all over the city. He crossed the bridge over to Ile St. Louis, an island in the river. He smiled. The city held reminders of Marie's husband as well.

He passed a wine bar and decided to go in. He sat at a table and sipped a glass of wine. Each time he thought about who she claimed to be, the more common sense told him that no, it was not possible. On the other hand, the more he thought of Marie, the more he wanted to get back to her. He had left so abruptly, and he realized now he might have really alarmed her. He threw a few coins on the table, left without finishing his wine, and hurried toward the apartment. With each step, he anticipated seeing her again.

He wanted to tell her he believed her, but he just couldn't. He decided to play it cool and not tell her how he felt. He knew to express his doubts again would upset her further, and he truly wanted to help her discover her true identity. As he put his key in the lock, he pictured her face, hoping she would be relieved to see him. He opened the door wide. The apartment was empty.

Chapter 15

Ben did a quick search of the apartment. His heart sank. Where could she have gone? He ran back to the bedroom. All her belongings were still there, except her bag. He sat down on the couch, disheartened. Although it wasn't that late, he couldn't believe she would leave the apartment alone. He glanced over to the door as if willing it to open and noticed the spare key was no longer hanging on the hook. He let out a sigh of relief, knowing there was a chance she would return. As he sat there, he thought about how much his feelings for her had grown. He was about to go out and look for her, when he heard a noise outside the door. He jumped up, threw the door open and shouted, "Where were you?"

"I don't know, where were you?" she laughed.

Ben was shocked. It wasn't Marie; it was his sister Diana!

"I'm in Paris for a few days, and I thought I'd surprise you. By the look on your face, I was successful."

"Oh, come in," Ben said, as he gave her a quick hug and kissed her cheeks. "I'm glad to see you, and yes, you did surprise me."

"Who were you expecting?" Diana asked. She was quite curious. *Could it be, Ben's finally found a girl?*

"A friend." Ben hated that he was suddenly pulled back into his regular life. He had gotten so used to Marie and her mysterious ways, he had been living in a dream world. He loved his sister and all, but the timing couldn't be worse.

Diana dropped her suitcase by the door and took off her leopard print coat. She was a striking beauty, tall and thin, with deep green eyes and long, dark brown hair, which she straightened to perfection daily. She was always full of surprises, unlike her brother, who was very predictable. She began chatting about her job and what she would be doing over the next few days. Ben could hardly focus on what she was saying. When she excused herself to use the restroom, he cringed. He knew what was coming.

When Diana exited the bathroom, she eyed Ben questioningly. She had seen Marie's things on the counter and her nightgown hanging on the back of the door. *Oh*, Ben thought, *things are quickly getting complicated.*

"So, something you want to tell me?"

Just as Ben was about to open his mouth, he heard a key being inserted in the door. In walked Marie. She was startled when she saw Diana. The three of them stood, staring at one another in awkward silence. Ben was relieved to see her, but suddenly the room felt very, very small.

"Diana, this is Marie. Marie, this is my sister, Diana."

The two women exchanged pleasantries, and then looked back at Ben. There was no use trying to hide it. He proceeded carefully. "Marie is a friend of mine. She's been staying with me a few days."

"Oh," said Diana looking curiously at Marie. "You know, you look very familiar. Have we met?"

"No," Marie stated flatly.

"Well, looks like you have a full house. Sorry, I guess my little surprise has interrupted your plans. I'll call Olivia. I'm sure I can crash at her place. If not, I can get a hotel. I'm on expenses you know."

She pulled her cell phone out of her coat pocket, and in short order, she was chatting with a friend from school. Marie stared at her, having no idea what this strange behavior was, talking into an object held up to her ear as if it was talking back to her. Diana smiled, "Ok, I'm all set, so I'll leave you two alone. I hope the three of us can meet for dinner while I'm in town so we can get to know one another."

"Of course," said Ben.

"Well then, I'll telephone you tomorrow afternoon. Nice to meet you Marie."

Before Ben closed the door, he mouthed a "thank you" to his sister. She smiled and winked. He knew she wouldn't mention this to anyone until they had a chance to talk, and for that, he was thankful. The fewer people he had to explain anything to, the better.

Closing the door, Ben turned and quietly said, "Where have you been?"

"I was afraid. I decided to go out and look for you."

"Oh, I didn't' mean to scare you, I just..." Ben shrugged.

"Is it all right? I mean, with your sister?"

"It will be fine. We'll figure all that out tomorrow. For how, I have to tell you something."

Marie felt nerves fluttering in her stomach. She had no idea what was coming, especially after Ben's unexpected departure. He led her over to the couch where they sat down together.

He smoothed her hair behind her ear absentmindedly. "For the past few days, I've listened to you and tried to help you in any way I can, even though what you claim is impossible to accept. Why you insist you are Marie Antoinette is a mystery to me, but it doesn't matter somehow. I don't understand how, or why, but I have faith that you've come into my life for a reason. I am here to help you."

Marie felt tears in her eyes as they sat next to each other for a while, listening to the fire crackling in the fireplace. Eventually, Ben got up and fixed them an omelet, toasted a baguette, and opened a bottle of wine to go with their dinner. After they ate, he went into the bathroom to get ready for bed. There on the back of the door hung Marie's nightgown, but something else caught his eye. From the same hook hung her rosary. He had noticed it before, peeking out from under her shirt or dress, but this was his first chance to have a good look at it. He carefully took it down. *What an exquisite piece,* he thought. It was a long, delicate gold chain necklace with diamonds and pearls interspersed at random between the gold links. At the bottom hung an oval medallion framed in gold filigree. Painted on the medallion was a miniature portrayal of the Virgin Mary. From the medallion, a six-inch length of chain dangled down independently with prayer beads evenly spaced to the end, where finally there hung a small ornate gold cross, embedded with more tiny diamonds and pearls. Puzzled, Ben wondered where a girl with so few belongings came to be in the possession of such an obviously expensive piece. He hung it back on the door and walked out.

Once again, Marie retired to Ben's room and he remained on the couch. He sat up for a long time that night staring into the fire, wondering what tomorrow would bring. He walked over to the bookshelf and removed the book on French history. He sat in the dim light, reading everything he could find about Marie Antoinette. He wanted to know everything. It might help him help Marie somehow.

Ben read for quite a long time, starting with her arrival at Versailles at age 14. She was quite young to be married, especially to a man she had never met. Her life was not easy. Throughout her time as dauphine, and then queen, she was accused often of things she did not do. From the Diamond Necklace Affair where she was accused of theft, to the shocking accusations of a scandalous sex life, she was gossiped about constantly. There was never any proof, but the French people of that time were miserable, and she became the scapegoat for all the things wrong in their lives. The worst accusations were the slanderous pamphlets that were spread around about her. They were nasty and graphic. *The political climate was ugly, even back then*, Ben thought.

He read on, skipping over the details of the revolution itself, focusing only on the parts having to do with Marie. He was fascinated by the story of an escape attempt that was made after they were in prison. It was of course, unsuccessful. It saddened him to read the account of all the time she spent in prison alone, after Louis was beheaded. On the following page, there was a painting of her, in her cell, toward the end of her life. She looked old. The starkness of it, compared to her life before, was astounding. Yes, Marie had wasted her life in some respects, and she was extravagant, but did she deserve... this?

He turned the page to the last day of her life. His heart pounded in his chest as he read a graphic description of the moments leading to her death: "She was led through town in an open cattle cart while people screamed insults and spit on her. As she was climbing the steps to the guillotine, she accidentally stepped on a guardsman's foot. She quietly said, 'Pardon.' She was her elegant and gracious self until the very end."

He closed the book. Many questions remained unanswered. He tried to put it all together in his mind. If the "Marie" sleeping in the next room was the same "Marie" from the history book, she's the "Marie" before any of the tragic events of her life had played out. She's here as a teenager... still a virgin. The book clearly states she and Louis did not consummate their marriage until she was in her twenties, after they had become king and queen. Ben knew Marie Antoinette was dead. Yet the woman with him claimed to be her. Would she somehow return to the past, so that history could play out as it had before? Was his friendship with her doomed, before it really got started? How much time did they have? He shook his head. *It's preposterous.* He opened the book again and absent-mindedly turned the pages. Then, he saw it—a painting of Marie Antoinette when she was young. There she was right in front of him, staring from the pages of the book, the same girl sleeping right in the next room.

Chapter 16

Ben woke early after a fitful night's sleep, immediately dreading the day. Diane had shown up the night before quite unexpectedly, and now they were supposed to meet for dinner. How in the world could he explain Marie to her?

All morning long he tried to focus on his work, but his mind wandered, not only about the impending dinner with Diana, but the painting he had seen of the young Marie Antoinette. It haunted him. He was thankful it was an uneventful morning with no emergency calls. He was relieved when afternoon came. His co-workers asked if he would like to eat lunch with them, but he declined. No one on his shift knew he had had further contact with the girl from the Louvre. Having to explain Marie to his sister was bad enough, but having to explain her to his colleagues would be impossible.

When he returned home, Marie was out on the terrace. She didn't hear him come in and he paused for a few moments, watching her. She was standing at the rail, staring out over the city. From the terrace, you could see the Seine in the distance and the tip of Notre Dame. He wondered what was going through her mind. Sensing him behind her, she turned, smiled, and nodded her head, inviting him to join her.

Without thinking it through, he walked right over to her, put his hand under her chin and lifted her face to his. She looked at him questioningly and he gently brushed his lips against hers. Her eyes opened wide and she immediately pushed back from him. "No Ben, you know this can't happen." She folded her arms around herself from the cold and went back in the apartment and sat on the couch.

Ben came inside, closing the door behind him. The apartment felt cold and dreary, just like the weather outside. He felt like a fool. "I'm sorry... I don't know what came over me. It won't happen again."

"Well, see that it doesn't." She had spoken in that haughty manner she sometimes had and instantly regretted it. No matter how she felt, Ben didn't deserve rudeness. She opened a book she found on the coffee table and pretended to read, while Ben busied himself with some paperwork at his desk. They were both lost in their own thoughts.

Sometime later, they discussed the dinner with Diana, and they both decided it was best if Marie stayed behind. It was too risky, and they didn't want to arouse suspicion that something wasn't quite right. When Ben called to set up a time to meet, he simply told Diana that Marie couldn't make it, that she had other plans.

Later that evening, Ben showered and shaved. As he splashed some cologne on his face, he noticed Marie's rosary reflected in the mirror, still on the hook behind him. He turned and gently took it down. He studied it as he had the previous day, but when he turned it over, he saw something he had not seen before. On the back of the medallion, in tiny engraving was an M and an A, intertwined with one another. He had seen that monogram last night in the history book. There was a close-up photograph of it embroidered on some bedding in Versailles. His first thought was to rush out of the room and demand Marie tell him where she got it. Then he froze. *Is this a replica of an old piece, or something more?*

Hands shaking, he dropped the rosary into his jacket pocket. He knew replicas of antique items existed. He also knew where he could have it evaluated. Excited and nervous at the same time, he decided not to tell Marie—not yet. *It's probably nothing*, he thought.

"I'll try and hurry dinner and return as soon as I can."

"Very well. Have a pleasant evening."

Ben paused before opening the door to leave. Marie looked over and smiled. *Thank goodness*, thought Ben, *if she was angry about the kiss, she seems to be over it now.*

His mind full of questions, he took the stairs two at a time and exited the apartment building. It was a short distance to the antique store he passed often on his neighborhood walks. When Ben approached the door, an elderly gentleman was coming out.

"Please sir, I have something I want to show you. Can you spare a few minutes?"

The man shrugged, opened the door and stood just inside. Ben carefully extracted the rosary from his pocket. The man took it in his hands and inspected it. He looked curiously at Ben and said, "Follow me." They walked together to a glass case near the back of the store. The man reached around and grabbed a loupe. In silence he carefully studied each diamond. He moved his way around the piece, stopped at the medallion and turned it over. Through the loupe he saw the monogram. Without looking up, he quietly spoke. "Where did you get this?"

Ben thought fast. "It's been passed down through my family for many years."

"Where did they get it?"

"I'm not sure."

The man eyed him suspiciously. "Sir, this rosary has historical significance. I would date it sometime in the late 18th century. Hold on a moment." With that, he disappeared behind a hanging curtain into a back room. He returned in a few moments with a large book. He flipped through the pages and suddenly stopped. "Look, here." He pointed to a photograph of a small painting. It was of a wedding ceremony. Under it the caption read, "Marriage between Louis XVI and Marie Antoinette of Austria, May 16, 1770." Ben looked up at the man, not understanding the significance of the picture. The man handed the loupe to Ben. "Here, look at the object hanging from the woman's hand, under the Bible."

Ben almost choked when he saw it—a rosary exactly like Marie's. The man continued speaking. "For over 200 years the whereabouts of this rosary has been a mystery. It was crafted especially for Marie Antoinette by the Mellerio family jewelers, and presented to her on her wedding day. It was mentioned in a letter she wrote to her mother, The Empress of Austria. Not many of Marie's things survived her, and this piece was assumed stolen from Versailles when it was ransacked after the king and queen were imprisoned. She had hoped it would be returned to her, but it was never recovered. You can imagine my curiosity as to its whereabouts all these years. By any chance, are you interested in selling it, or possibly donating it? It should be in a museum."

Ben kept his cool. "That is a decision I can't make on my own. I'll have to speak to my family. How confident are you that this rosary is authentic?"

"I am as confident as I've ever been in my 45 years of being in this business. However, if you are comfortable leaving it with me, I could take it to a colleague for a second opinion."

Ben shook his head. "No, I'm not leaving it."

"Of course. Would you mind waiting while I call him? He lives right around the corner. Maybe he can see us now."

"Okay, but you will have to make it quick, I have a dinner date to get to."

"I'm Frédéric by the way."

"I'm Ben."

As Frédéric walked back behind the curtain, Ben's knees were knocking. He felt sure he would faint if he didn't get out of the shop right away. He could not hear the phone conversation behind the curtain. He considered leaving, but he felt his whole life hung on the confirmation of the information he had just received. He glanced at his watch as the man came back.

"He'll be here in five minutes."

"Okay," said Ben, "Excuse me a moment, won't you?"

"Surely."

Ben stepped out of the shop and called his sister to tell her he was running a few minutes late. As soon as he hung up, he saw a middle-aged man coming toward him at a quick pace. The man paused as Ben opened the door. They entered the shop and walked together to the back. The man introduced himself, "I'm Jean-Paul. Are you the gentleman with the item?"

"Yes, I am."

Frédéric didn't speak, but handed Jean-Paul the loupe and the rosary. He scrutinized it just as his friend had, and then looked down at the book, still open to the photo of the painting of Marie's wedding day. He shook his head, mumbling to himself, "It can't be." Finally, he turned to Ben. "It's incredible. A piece of this magnitude, thought lost all these years, is here, in my hand. It's inconceivable!"

Ben slowly put his hand out to receive the rosary back. "So, it's your opinion that this piece is authentic?"

"Unquestionably."

Ben took the rosary from Jean-Paul and dropped it in his pocket. "Thank you so much for your time and for your assessment. I will speak to my family and be in touch."

Frédéric gave him one of his business cards and said, "We look forward to hearing from you."

With that, Ben turned and hurried out the door. He didn't want any further questions. He raced through the streets blindly. *How can this be*?

Ben had no idea how he would get through dinner. *I'll have to make small talk and act like nothing is wrong. I have to get back to Marie as quickly as I can.* He saw Diana sitting outside the café, and waved at her from a distance. *I must act normal*, he thought.

He unwrapped the scarf around his neck as he sat down. "Sorry I'm late."

"It's okay. I just ordered Beef Bourguignon for each of us. I hope that suits you."

"Thank you, that will be fine."

"You seem preoccupied. Is anything wrong?"

"No, just rushing around I guess."

"How is your friend, Marie?"

Ben looked down, feeling self-conscious. "She's fine."

"Have you known her long? Are the two of you together?"

"Oh no. It isn't anything like that. Jake, one of my coworkers introduced us. She's new in town and I offered for her to stay with me until she finds an apartment. You know how difficult that can be in Paris."

"How cozy."

"No, not really. I gave her my room, just like I do when you're in town."

"So... just friends?"

"Yes... just friends."

"You're hopeless, Ben. And you're getting old."

"Not too old though, right?"

"Right." She considered pressing further, but didn't. If there were more to the relationship than he was letting on, she'd find out soon enough.

"Well, I'm off to London tomorrow. It was great seeing you, even for this short time."

"It was great to see you too, little sister," Ben said, teasing her affectionately.

Diana giggled. "Promise me we'll spend more time together on my next trip to Paris. Don't worry, I'll be sure to call ahead next time and give you some warning. Maybe I'll even get a chance to become better acquainted with Marie."

"Perhaps." Ben quickly paid the check, they kissed goodbye on both cheeks, and went their separate ways.

He hurried toward the apartment. He couldn't wait to see Marie, but he had no idea what he would say to her. With the revelation of the rosary, her story began to sound more plausible. He wanted so badly to believe her, to have faith in her, but the idea of her traveling through time was outrageous. He couldn't let his growing feelings for her make him believe something that wasn't possible.

Then his mind took another turn. He imagined having a romantic encounter with her when he returned, wondering what their first real kiss would be like. The thought aroused him and he quickened his steps. Regardless of her reaction to the first kiss, he held out hope.

When he opened the door, his heart sank. The apartment was dark and the bedroom door was closed. Evidently, she was already asleep. Ben was disappointed and considered waking her, but chose not to. What he didn't know was that Marie was lying awake in the next room, staring into the darkness. The brief kiss had confused her. To add romance to her already complicated situation seemed ridiculous... and yet her body had responded in a way she wasn't used to. Wishing she had not been so rude, she tossed and turned. When she heard Ben come in, she remained still and quiet until she was sure he thought she was asleep.

This was Ben's fourth night spent on the couch. He didn't mind usually, but tonight it bothered him. She had gone to bed without so much as a goodnight. She must have been more offended over the kiss than he thought. He yearned to tell her about the rosary but since she was already asleep, he would have to wait.

He turned on a lamp and decided to read until he got sleepy, but he couldn't keep his mind focused. He felt edgy, unsettled. He finally came up with a plan. Tomorrow he would give Marie a special day, a day where they could roam the streets of Paris, not worrying about the past or the future. He felt she would be glad to get out, happy for the distraction. Maybe then he would find the perfect moment to tell her about the rosary.

Chapter 17

When Marie emerged from the bedroom the next morning, Ben was busy making coffee.

"Oh, I didn't expect to see you here. Don't you have to go to work?"

"No, I called in and asked someone take my shift."

"How was your dinner with Diana last night?"

"Fine, just fine. She didn't ask too many questions." Ben hesitated just a moment and continued. "I want to take you out today. I want to show you some of my favorite places."

"Oh… well… that would be nice, although I love it here. It's so quiet and peaceful."

"You know, I think it would do us both some good to get out and have a little fun. The past few days have been intense, to say the least."

"Yes, it's been quite intense, hasn't it?" Marie sighed deeply. "I have to ask you… are you sorry you got involved with me? First at the Louvre, and then by the bench on the river?"

Ben walked over to her and gently put his arm around her. "No, I'm not sorry. I'm glad." Ben decided to be completely honest with her, and as he spoke, he realized he was being honest with himself as well. "From the first moment I saw you in the

Louvre, I felt something. At first, I thought it was just pity, but really, it was more..." Ben's voice trailed off.

"Ben... I have never been in love, not like I dreamed it would be. Louis is kind and sweet, and would do anything for me, but that's where it ends. As for you and me, I'm sure you understand my position. I am a married woman. I do not know why I am here, or for how long. I have no idea what even brought me here in the first place."

"I don't know either, but this is where you are for now. Why don't we go out and enjoy this day... as friends?" Ben wanted to tell her she was brought here to meet him, to fall in love, and have the happiness she deserved, but he remained silent.

They dressed and left the apartment. They wandered the streets of Paris, occasionally stepping into a shop or a gallery to look around. They ended up at Place Des Vosges, a beautiful square built in the early 1600's by King Henry IV. The day was sunny and unseasonably warm, and they entered the square through the triple arches. Walking all the way around the open-air passageways, they eventually settled on a bench in the middle of the lawn. They were totally relaxed and talked nonstop, more at ease with one another today than at any other time since they met. They spoke of many things, focusing mainly on the here and now, the people around them, and their surroundings. Marie tried her best not to talk of the past, but it was difficult for her. Right in the center of the square stood a statue of King Louis XIII, sitting proudly on his horse. No matter where they turned, there were reminders of the past, of the world she came from.

After a while, they decided to continue walking. The sun was high in the sky and they began discussing lunch plans. Turning the next corner, Marie stopped in front of a building noticing the sign, Musée Carnavalet. "What kind of museum is this?" Marie asked as she pointed to the sign.

"I'm not sure. I've never been inside."

"Let's go in."

"I don't know Marie..."

"Please Ben. I'm curious. Let's go!"

For some reason, Ben had an uneasy feeling, but he couldn't put his finger on why. Eventually Marie's sudden carefree demeanor persuaded him and they went inside.

Entering through the large wooden doors on the ground floor, they passed through an inner courtyard of intricately sculpted topiaries and hedges. They learned the museum was made up of two townhomes, previously the home of two aristocratic families in the 17th century, before the Court moved to Versailles. This information really peaked Marie's interest. The rooms and hallways throughout held paintings, furniture, and various artifacts from the original founding of Paris in 4600 BC to the present day. The exhibits were not laid out in chronological order, so one never knew what was around the next corner. The museum was practically empty, so they could explore each area at their leisure.

Once upstairs, the exhibits took on a special interest to them both, as they had entered an area of the late 1700's, Marie's time. They continued in silence, and Ben observed her manner change from that of carefree interest to careful scrutiny of everything she saw.

When they turned down the next hallway, she whispered, "My God," and froze. A moment later, she began walking, trance-like, down the hall and stopped in front of an exquisite handmade inlay writing desk. Ben paused just behind her and waited. "This is my writing table. I… I… can't believe it. I sat at this very desk and wrote a letter to my mother the night before everything changed." Ben watched as she carefully crossed over the golden rope cordoning off the desk. Expertly, she reached behind it and slipped out a piece of wood perfectly carved into back of the desk, impossible to detect if you didn't know it was there. From the hidden compartment, she retrieved a piece of paper folded into thirds, then shoved the small block of wood back into place. Seconds later she was back on the other side of rope, her hands shaking.

"Is that the letter?" asked Ben.

"Yes, it is."

"Shall we open it?"

"Will you do it for me? I'm…" Marie's voice trailed off. Standing there in the deserted hallway, Ben took the letter and turned it over. There on the back was a dark red wax seal, with her monogram embedded into it—the exact monogram that was engraved on the rosary. Now Ben's hands began to shake. He looked up into her eyes, and in that moment, he believed her. There was no doubt remaining that standing before him was the real Marie Antoinette.

He tried to compose himself before he spoke, but instead he just blurted it out. "Marie, I believe you… I mean, I believe you are here from another time. I don't understand it, it doesn't make sense, but I believe you. I also have a confession to make.

Last night, I took your rosary to a shop that specializes in antique jewelry. Two different experts looked at it, and confirmed that it was a rosary that once belonged to you." He paused and waited for a reaction, and when she remained silent, he continued. "I'm so sorry I didn't believe you before. I should have."

Marie's eyes glazed over with tears. The impact of the letter had been profound, and she found herself flooded with peace, now that she knew Ben finally believed her. She realized the letter he held in his hand was the final piece of the puzzle. "I understand. I feel relieved, so thankful that you believe me now. I don't think we'll ever understand how, or why, but I am thankful to have you here, now, in my life." They embraced for a brief moment, then another couple entered the hallway. "Can we leave now?"

"Yes, let's go someplace where we can talk."

They began to make their way through the other rooms, following the signs to the exit. They had no idea they were about to walk into an area dedicated to the French Revolution. Ben saw the sign ahead, and felt sick to his stomach. *No... not now!* Only a few moments ago they had been so happy, and now this. He wanted to turn them around, but Marie had already seen it. She turned and looked at him helplessly.

"Let's just get through there as quickly as we can. Keep your eyes straight ahead," Ben said.

They rushed through the large room, and when they entered the next smaller room, Marie looked up, thinking the revolution exhibits were over. She scanned the area for the exit, and there on the far wall a painting caught her eye. Ben was trying to lead her out, but she stopped. She stared into the eyes of the man in the painting, and under it read the words, MAXIMILIEN ROBESPIERRE – INFLUENTIAL LEADER OF THE FRENCH REVOLUTION. She didn't recognize the name, but the face... she felt she had seen it before. Fear pulsed through her body when it came to her. He looked remarkably like the man she had seen at the gates of Versailles, the train station, and by the Seine the night she went with Ben. *Don't be silly*, she thought, *you didn't get a good look at him through the rain, or in the dark. It can't be.*

"What is it? What's wrong?" said Ben.

"It's nothing, let's go." Although Marie knew Ben now believed she was who she claimed to be, to tell him that she thought she had seen another person from the past would be too much. She would keep the thought to herself for now. She regained her composure as they walked down the marble staircase, through the exit, and back onto the street.

Chapter 18

Everything changed with the discovery of the letter. Ben and Marie left the museum, crossed the street, and entered the first café they came to. Both were eager to talk. As soon as they settled into their seats, Ben hesitantly started to speak. "Marie, I'm sorry... the letter... makes it all so real."

"How do you feel about it?"

"I don't know. I never thought such a thing was possible, but here you sit, right in front of me."

"You really believe me? You no longer have doubts?"

"No, no doubts."

"You have no idea the relief I feel, hearing you say that. May I see the letter?"

Ben passed it over, and she carefully cracked the seal, but stopped before unfolding it. She handed the letter back to Ben. "Why don't you take it, and I'll tell you what it says."

"That isn't necessary. I told you I believe you."

"I know, but I feel it's important. Doubts may come again, and I want to preempt any uncertainties that may come up in the future."

"Okay, go ahead." Ben scanned the letter as Marie described its contents. She remembered everything with remarkable accuracy. She expressed in the letter how much she missed Austria and her family, how she was trying her best to please Louis and the others at court every day. She described her elegant birthday party in great detail. It was sweet, almost juvenile in nature, and by the end of it, Ben felt he understood her world as never before. She was desperate for approval, from her new family, as well as the one she left behind. He gently handed the letter back to her.

Her hand quivered as she looked it over. It felt strange for her to hold the now yellowed, fragile parchment she had written on just days ago. The ink had faded considerably, but she could still make out her signature and the date at the bottom, November 8, 1773. Carefully folding it up, she gave it back to Ben, "Please keep this safe until we get back to the apartment."

"I will," he said, as he put it in his jacket pocket. "I do have a question though. Why was it hidden away like that, in a secret compartment?"

"Because there are prying eyes and spies all over Versailles. I only trust one person to see that my letters are delivered to Austria without being opened. I hid it away until I would see him the next day."

"See who?"

"Count Mercy. He was sent to France to assist me, at least that is what I was told. I now know from reading the history book that he was observing me closely and informing my mother of my every move. I always found her insight uncanny, now I know why. I feel betrayed." Looking around the room she continued, "I don't actually feel much like dining. Not right now. May we leave?"

"Of course."

They exited the café and began walking in silence, each pondering the events of the day. They walked quite far, all the way to the Tuileries Gardens. They settled on a bench off by itself, dappled in sunlight peeking through the trees. The walk had done them good, as they both had time to settle in and acknowledge their new relationship of trust and acceptance. No longer were they two individuals, they had a unique bond that brought them closer than they ever expected.

A young couple passed by pushing a baby stroller, while their other two children played chase, weaving in and out of the trees across the way. Marie laughed. "That brings back memories."

"Of what?"

"It reminds me of something that happened when I was a child."

"Go on..." Ben said, leaning toward her.

"I was about seven or eight years old and Mozart had come to Vienna to perform for my family. He was about my age, and after the concert, we ran around the palace, playing chase with the other children. At one point, he slipped on the wood floor, and would've fallen, but I caught him just in time."

"That's incredible! You played with Mozart?" Ben shook his head. "I can't imagine the life you've had."

"Those were my happiest days, living with my family in the palace. The day they sent me off to France, I had no idea what was ahead. I was young... so naïve at 14. I still remember that day, vividly. I hugged my mother goodbye and as my carriage rolled away, I watched her, standing there, until she was no longer in sight. I felt betrayed." Marie looked down, studying the intricate ironwork of the bench. "I knew she loved me, but she loved her country more. The further I got from Austria, the more determined I became to be the best I could be for France, and make my mother proud. She used me to secure peace between the two countries, and I was desperate to do all I could do to assist that. I had no idea how ill-prepared I was."

Marie paused, her eyes fixed straight ahead. "When we arrived at the border of Austria and France, they took everything I had away from me. They took all my clothes and shoes, my jewelry, my books, everything. They even took... they even took my dog away. I never saw him again. I crossed into France without a single possession—nothing. I was not allowed to bring a keepsake of my country, my family, or my childhood. It was like a death... the death of my innocence, of my beautiful, lovely life. Everything changed that day.

"As we rode deeper and deeper into the French countryside, I felt myself becoming a different person. I buried that happy little girl in my heart. I found courage. Deep inside me, it welled up. By the time I was presented to Louis, my future husband, I was determined. Determined to be agreeable, sweet, and kind. Maybe that's part of the reason I ended up the way I did. As I think about it now, with full knowledge of how I handled myself, I don't think I really did bury that little girl. I had to grow up so quickly, and when my affection to Louis was not returned, maybe I retreated back to that little girl, and the childhood I loved and missed so much." Happy memories, sad memories, they were all there. Now Marie had a second chance at life and wondered how she would handle it. The leaves rustled overhead. "Oh, I am so sorry. I've talked too much. Why didn't you stop me?"

"Because you're fascinating. I want to know all there is to know about you. Historians don't always get it right. To read about Marie Antoinette is one thing, but to have her... you... sitting in front of me, let's just say, it's... extraordinary."

"We always seem to talk about me, and you already know so much. But I know very little about you. Why don't you tell me something from your childhood, a favorite memory perhaps?"

"Well, let's see." Ben smiled. "My memories aren't nearly as interesting as playing with Mozart, but I'll try. Oh, I know. One summer my father took my sister and me to Capri on holiday. We stayed on the island in a house my father leased for an entire month. We had a great time. I think I was about nine years old. The house stood on the side of a cliff, overlooking the Mediterranean. I can still picture the colors of the water. It was breathtaking. I spent every moment I could outside.

"One afternoon, I was sleeping on a hammock in the backyard. I awoke to a buzzing sound. I opened my eyes and saw a very large bumblebee buzzing around my head. When I tried to get out of the hammock, I got all tangled up in the ropes. As I frantically tried to get untangled, the bee stung me, right on the tip of my nose. It was so painful I started to cry, and as I finally freed myself from the ropes, the hammock flipped over, and I landed flat on the ground! The worst part? There was a pretty young girl about my age that lived next door and as I limped back up to the house, I saw her standing over in her yard, laughing hysterically. I was so embarrassed."

"Whatever happened?"

"We became best friends a few days later, and actually, she was the first girl to ever give me a kiss."

"That's wonderful!" Marie said enthusiastically. "See, you do have interesting stories to tell." She looked at Ben and paused before going on. "Do you want to hear about my first *real* kiss?"

"I don't know... will it make me jealous?"

"I don't think so." She hesitated just a moment, looked down, and softly said, "It was yesterday, with you."

Ben smiled mischievously. "That wasn't a *real* kiss." He paused before going on. "Didn't Louis ever kiss you?"

"He tried... I mean, he did... but when you kissed me, it was different," Marie whispered, "in so many ways. I can't explain it."

"Can you try?"

"No. Let's go. Suddenly, I'm hungry."

Ben walked her over to a food stand at the garden's entrance, and bought them each a ham and cheese crepe. They ate while leaning against a stone embankment and as Marie looked around, she saw something curious off in the distance. "What is that structure over there?"

Ben looked up and saw the tip of the Eiffel Tower. Immediately he had an idea. "It's called the Eiffel Tower. Would you like to see it up close?"

"Could we?"

"We can. It will be dark soon. It's the perfect time to go."

"In the dark? I don't understand."

"You will," said Ben, smiling a mysterious smile.

He guided her to the nearest metro station, and they were off. His heart skipped a beat just thinking about her reaction as they got off the metro at Champ-De-Mars. As they walked, as if out of nowhere, the tower came into view, rising straight up from the ground. Ben had brought her in right at the base of the structure. Marie was stunned at the enormity of it. She had never seen anything this massive in her entire life. Standing under it, and looking directly up through the center, Marie lost her balance. They laughed as Ben caught her just as she was about to topple over. They strolled around amongst the crowd, enjoying the party-like atmosphere. There were animated tourists, various musicians hoping for a coin or two, jugglers, and vendors selling mini replicas of the tower, decorative scarves, and tiny key chains.

Ben glanced at his watch. He had a surprise to finish this astonishing day with flare. He led Marie away from the tower, over a bridge, across the Seine, and up a long gradual incline. By the time they climbed several flights of stairs and reached the top of the hill at Trocadéro, the tower glowed with the golden radiance it takes on at dusk each evening. When Ben turned her around, for the first time she saw the entire monument from top to bottom in all its glory. She was completely mesmerized. He had taken her to the perfect spot—the best view in the city.

As Ben's watch reached exactly 5:00, he watched Marie's face as she gazed at the tower in the distance. Instantaneously, thousands of golden lights began to twinkle rapidly. Never in her life had she seen anything so spectacular. The beauty of the moment overwhelmed them both.

Ben cautiously leaned in and kissed her. It was a tender kiss at first, but it grew in intensity as Marie responded longingly. An icy wind swirled up around them, their minds swirling as well. They knew at that moment, that no matter what happened in the past, the present, or the future, their hearts would be forever intertwined. The kiss ended and as Ben pulled back and looked at her, she smiled and laid her head on his chest, and for the first time, she felt completely relaxed, and safe.

They continued to watch the tower sparkle, and in a few minutes, it returned to its original golden glow. Now that the sun had set, the entire city had taken on a sepia-tone, ancient and mysterious. For the first time in his life, Ben understood why Paris was considered the most romantic city in the world. He was living it. He would never forget this day, or this evening. It was absolutely perfect.

When they returned to the apartment, they collapsed on the couch, both exhausted. Exhausted in body, but not in spirit. There was anticipation in the air. Marie excused herself to the bathroom and shut the door. She stared into the mirror, questions racing through her mind. She knew what Ben wanted, she also knew she wanted the same thing. She rinsed her face and brushed her hair. She knew she was stalling, but she was afraid. She had no idea what was going to happen. Finally she emerged from the bathroom.

Ben took the lead, and before long they were in a passionate kiss. There was no hesitation anymore, for either of them. Marie had no experience with a man wanting her. It was scary, but wonderful at the same time. Her mind lost all logical thought, and her body responded with intensity. Within moments they were on the couch. Desires grew, neither one thinking about the possible consequences of their actions. At one point, Marie's inexperience caused her to hesitate, and as Ben searched her eyes... he remembered.

"You've never been with a man before. How do you feel about this?"

As soon as he spoke, he regretted it. His words had snatched the passion from the air. Marie immediately stood up, walked over by the doors, looking out over the city, speaking with her back to him. "My feelings for you are strong. I've never had these feelings for a man before. It's confusing, but it feels right." She turned to face him. "But there's the question of my duty, my future. I hope you understand."

Ben let out his breath. "I understand. I don't like it, but I understand." Frustrated, he picked up their coffee cups left from the morning and walked over to the sink. Marie knew she had hurt him, but hoped she hadn't angered him. Perhaps a small concession was in order.

"Ben, I know we haven't known each other but a few days, but I would like it very much if you would sleep with me in your bed tonight."

"Sleep?" Ben asked in a disappointed tone.

"Yes, sleep. But I want you close to me."

"Okay, I can handle it, for now..." He winked at her, adding a bit of playfulness. She could feel how much he wanted her, but he was willing to wait. For that, she was grateful.

Together in Ben's bed should have felt awkward, but it did not. It was as if they had known each other for years. Deep down inside, they both knew they were destined to be together. As long as Marie was here, she would stay with Ben. As they drifted off to sleep, they snuggled closer and closer against the cold.

Chapter 19

Ben and Marie fell into a routine over the next few days. While he was at work, she would stay at the apartment reading, watching TV, or sitting on the balcony writing. She had picked up a handmade journal and an ornate pen in one of the shops in their neighborhood, and had started to write down her thoughts every day. It helped her cope with all the changes that had occurred in her life. She was happy with Ben, but she was a woman out of her element, out of her century, and it still overwhelmed her at times. Ben never asked to read the journal, although the temptation was there. He knew it contained her private thoughts and he respected that.

When Ben wasn't at work, they enjoyed each other's company, either in the apartment, or walking the streets of Paris. They maintained a level of comfort with their situation, but the future was unknown. Usually, they chose not to discuss it. Their physical relationship intensified despite Marie's uneasiness, even though they had done nothing but sleep in the same bed.

One morning Marie glanced at the calendar hanging on the kitchen wall and realized she had arrived just over a week ago. It was hard to believe. It seemed much longer to her. She felt she had lived a lifetime since she awoke that fateful morning in her bed at Versailles. On this particular day, seeing the calendar unsettled her for some reason. For the rest of the day she had a dark, ominous feeling that she could not shake. She tried to busy herself, but continued to be distracted. As the day wore on, she felt heaviness with each breath she took. She couldn't wait for Ben to get home, sure his presence would ease her mind.

As soon as he walked in the door she commented, "Do you realize it's been over a week since I got here?"

"Wow... it seems longer... in a good way." He smiled at her as he hung his coat on the hook. He walked into the bathroom to take a shower and change clothes.

"Yes, of course." Her voice trailed off. Marie continued to feel anxious. Somewhere deep down in her soul, she was beginning to feel different, unsure, awkward even. She shook those feelings off and went over to the kitchen to prepare their evening meal, a dinner of pasta with a creamy mushroom sauce, and a green salad. Ben had been teaching her a few things in the kitchen. She found cooking therapeutic. As she finished up and brought the steaming plates of pasta to the table, Ben came out of the bedroom, relaxed and happy.

"This looks amazing. Smells good too."

Marie was sad that her mood did not match his, but she couldn't help it. She managed a smile. Ben didn't seem to notice her low spirit as he talked about his day and the people he had assisted. He found it such a comfort to come home to her. He loved having someone to share his day with.

They watched a little TV after dinner, and Ben began to notice Marie's behavior. Normally she was quite inquisitive about whatever show they were watching, trying to learn all she could. Tonight, she was quiet... a million miles away. It made him uncomfortable.

Later when they got into bed, she rolled over, facing the wall, and stayed that way. The past haunted her mind. As much as she wanted to stay in the present, her thoughts kept taking her back. She had adjusted to her contemporary life with Ben and wished it were enough. It had seemed so until today. The eerie feeling stayed with her until she fell asleep.

Chapter 20

Ben sat straight up in bed when the screaming started. He reached for Marie in the darkness, held her tight, and repeated her name over and over. After what seemed like an eternity the nightmare ended and Marie woke up, sobbing. He continued holding her as she tried to settle down.

"It's only a dream, it's only a dream," Ben said, as he rocked her back and forth.

"It... was... horrible... I was being chased. A mob was chasing me through the darkness in the forest near Versailles. They kept screaming at me, but I couldn't understand what they were saying. They kept getting closer and closer. I hid in some bushes and soon they surrounded me. They couldn't see me, but I could hear the ugly, hideous things they were saying. They wanted me dead. They said they would find my children and eat them alive. I began vomiting. They heard me. They grabbed me..." Her voice trailed off as Ben continued to cradle her in his arms.

"It's okay now, you're safe here, with me."

"Ben, it's not okay, not at all. What if I end up back there? What's keeping me here in the first place? What's going to happen?"

"I don't know, I can't read the future, so I can't tell you. All I know to be true, is that you are here, now. We are happy together. You are safe. No one can harm you."

"But the dream was so real Ben. It was like I was really there. It was... gruesome."

Ben didn't know what else to say. They lay there together, him stroking her arm and holding her tight until the sun came up. Somehow in the light of day, things seemed better, calmer. Ben got up and dressed for work.

"Will you be okay if I go to work?"

"Yes, I'm better now. Maybe I'll take a bath and rest. I'm tired. It was a long night."

"Are you sure? I can call in sick if I need to."

"No, I'll be fine. I promise."

"All right then, I'll be home by noon."

He closed the door and stood in the hall, not sure if he should leave her, even for a few hours. Reluctantly, he turned and left.

She didn't linger. She felt edgy, full of anxiety. She needed to get out, walk around, and release some of the tension she felt in her bones. Barely stopping to swallow a sip of coffee, she grabbed the key from the hook, and headed out the door.

At this early hour, the streets were practically deserted. Very few people were out. Marie walked blindly, not paying attention to where she was going, her mind full of thoughts about her life if she were to return to the past. She felt dizzy, but continued walking, hard and fast, as if she were late to an appointment. An appointment... with destiny.

"*Why am I here? What is my life to become? Should I desire to return to my time, even though I know my horrible fate?*" These and other questions spun out of control. Block after block went by as she continued to travel. Finally, exhausted in mind and spirit, she stopped and leaned against a concrete barrier that stood between her and the bank of the river below.

Her eyes rested on the building straight ahead, the Conciergerie. Her heart began beating wildly in her chest. She was staring directly at her future home, the tower prison. She would be moved here, after being held prisoner in the Tuileries. This is where she would reside until her execution. It seemed unfathomable that she could go from being the queen of France residing at Versailles, to this. *I don't understand. What happens to cause this in a few short years? Is extravagance enough to justify my death?* It was apparent from reading history that the leaders of the revolution hated the aristocracy. *But why? Surely there has to be more to it.*

She stood staring at the Conciergerie, feeling drawn to it. There was a strange pull in her heart to cross the bridge, go inside, and see it for herself. As if moved by an invisible force, she stepped forward. *I must face this,* she thought. If she was to continue living in the future and have a real life, she had to make sense of her past, even a past she had not lived yet. With sureness of step, she swiftly crossed over the bridge and stood in front of the building, noticing how different it was than the prison she remembered seeing when in Paris years before. Other structures had been added, but three of the original towers still stood.

Slowly she made her way around the building, until she saw an unoccupied entrance. The large wooden doors were open and with no one around, she walked right in. Partway down the massive center corridor, she saw a group of people. She walked over and stood with them. When a tour guide arrived, she listened closely and decided to follow the group, pretending to bc on the tour with the others.

It was a damp, dark, and dreary place. When she heard the guide mention her name, it startled her at first. She expected everyone to turn and look at her. *Of course, they don't know me.* But as the tour continued, it seemed she was the main reason the group came on the tour, a major point of interest. As they turned left down a dimly lit passageway, the guide continued talking about her, and not in a flattering way. Not wanting to hear the insults, she hung back, and when the rest of the tour moved forward, she turned right. The corridor sharply turned again, and in the dim light she saw a sign with an arrow pointing forward to THE CELL OF MARIE ANTOINETTE. She immediately wanted to run, to get out of there, but morbid curiosity took over. She couldn't stop. She had to see it through to the end. She continued down the corridor until she arrived at the cell. She peered through the bars into the dingy room. The wallpaper was ripped and faded. There was a crude wooden desk and chair on one side, and a small wooden bed on the other, made up with cheap fabrics.

An eerie, uneasy feeling came over her. Sitting at a desk facing the wall was a mannequin dressed in black. It was supposed to be her. One part of her wanted to run, the other part of her wanted to protest, to tell the others it was all wrong, that she wasn't guilty. She quickly stepped away from the area and continued to follow the passageway. Exiting the building, she entered a fenced-in outer courtyard and read a plaque she noticed hanging on the gate. It stated that it was here prisoners were allowed to say goodbye to their family, before being loaded onto an open cart and taken to the guillotine. She could not fathom it.

Just as she was about to exit through the gate, she sensed someone behind her. His hot breath tickled the back of her neck as he spoke, "You *will* return to face your accusers, Madame Antoinette. I will make sure of it." She didn't move, paralyzed by fear. When she heard the gravel crunch behind her, she turned just in time to see the man in black walking back into the building.

Trembling from head to toe she called out, "Who are you? Where do you come from?" He did not answer, and quickly disappeared around the corner. She followed him, but when she went around the corner, he had disappeared into the maze of the dark and dreary corridors of the Conciergerie.

A new layer of fear flooded her mind. Emotionally exhausted, she turned around, left through the gate, and started for home. Distraught, she became disoriented, not remembering the way back to the apartment. She stopped a moment to get her bearings and off in the distance she saw the tip of the Eiffel Tower. Her evening there with Ben flashed through her mind. The contrast of Paris that night, and Paris this morning left her feeling wounded. When she got to the apartment, she stretched out on the sofa with a cold cloth over her forehead.

Chapter 21

Ben came in from work and found Marie asleep on the couch. She stirred slightly as he crossed the room, and slowly opened her eyes. She looked at him intently, then closed her eyes and drifted back to sleep. "Marie?" She did not move. *Odd*, he thought, *she looked straight through me.*

He sat down across the room from her, trying to figure out what was going on. Her dream last night troubled him. He feared she was slipping back to the Marie he met over a week ago at the Louvre: the scared, distrustful Marie. The prospect troubled him. He was in love with her; he wanted her with all his heart. He wanted her to stay here, with him, and live out the rest of their lives together.

Even as those thoughts crossed his mind, he knew it was next to impossible. Once they came out of their self-imposed bubble, they would have to explain things. The two of them would not be able to continue living as if they were on an island. Sooner or later, there would be questions from family, co-workers, and friends. They would want to know all about her. *What will we say?* Ben shuddered again when he thought of her nightmare last night. He had never seen anyone so distraught.

Finally, she began to stir. She shook her head back and forth, "No, no, it's not true!" she whispered. "Take me, but leave my children alone." He knew she was having another nightmare so he tentatively sat down next to her on the couch and stroked her hair. He decided to wake her before the dream got worse. He gently shook her shoulder, calling her name, and finally she opened her eyes, and without expression, stared into his. He held his breath.

"Oh, it's you. For a moment, I wasn't sure where I was."

"What do you mean?"

"I just mean... I was confused for a moment." She closed her eyes, her forehead tensed. "I had another dream, back in my time. Why do you think this is happening now? I didn't have these dreams when I first got here."

"I'm not sure." He held her hands gently. "Is there anything I can get you? A glass of water? Something to eat?"

"No. I feel..." Marie hesitated to tell Ben the rest, but she felt she had to. She needed to be honest with him. He was all she had. "I... I went somewhere this morning."

"Where?"

"I went for a walk. I had no plan, nowhere to go, I just had to get out of the apartment. I felt anxious, like something was about to happen, but I didn't know what. I roamed the streets absentmindedly. When I finally stopped, I was standing directly across the river from the Conciergerie, the Tower Prison where I spend my last days.

"As I stood there, looking at it, something drew me in. I felt compelled to go inside and once there, I saw the cell where I was imprisoned before my death. It was ghastly. There was a grotesque statue of me, dressed in black, facing the wall." It was difficult for her to go on, but she had to get it all out. "I do not understand why people come to see such a thing all these years later. It's as if I'm a character in a book, but I am not, Ben, I'm real." She slowly continued, "Is it possible to change things? If I went back, could I change the outcome? Could I save my husband? My children? Could I save my own life? The possibilities haunt me. I feel..."

Ben interrupted. "Why are you thinking like this now? You aren't there... you're here. Even if you wanted to go back, how could you? You don't even know how you got here in the first place."

"I know, I know, but all these thoughts keep coming into my head. At first, as we grew closer and closer to one other, I was content. Content to stay here with you and never look back. But I can't deny these feelings, my sense of duty to my position. Do you think that will pass with time?"

"I don't know..." Ben's voice trailed off. He was lost in his own thoughts. He was afraid of what Marie was saying—afraid he was going to lose her. But did he really even have her? Could she give herself over to him fully as long as the past was between them?

"I don't know what the future holds, or the past for that matter. I can't fully grasp our situation, but I want you to know I've loved you almost from the first moment I saw you. That's got to be worth something." Ben paused a moment, carefully weighing his words before he went on. "I know you have feelings for me too. We could have a life together. Sooner or later you will adjust, I feel certain of it. I will be here for you, every step of the way."

"I know. You've been so patient, so understanding." Marie sat up looking at him anxiously, "There's more... something else I have to tell you."

Ben took a deep breath, not liking the tone of her voice, and asked, "What? What is it?"

"I fear there may be someone else here from my time. At first, I wasn't sure, but now, I'm certain."

"Who? What are you talking about?"

"That first day at Versailles, when the palace was empty, I ran out to the front gates to try to get out. They were locked. I dropped to the ground in the rain, and out of nowhere a man appeared. When he asked if I needed help, I turned and ran."

"Why do you think he's from the past?"

"Because I've seen him three times since then. At the train station when I left Versailles for Paris, he was there. We locked eyes for a moment... he seemed to know me. I looked away and when I looked back, he was gone. Then that night, when you found me by the river, he was there, standing in the shadows. When he stepped out, I ran. That's why I went with you to your apartment. I was frightened and felt I had no choice."

"Have you seen him since then?"

"Not until today."

"What? Where?"

"At the Conciergerie, in the outer courtyard."

"Did he speak to you?"

"Yes. He said, 'You *will* return to face your accusers, Madame Antoinette. I will make sure of it.' His voice was so sinister, so definite."

Ben sat back, shocked by what he just heard. *Could Marie be in danger?* This thought had never occurred to him.

"There's one more thing. I believe I saw a painting of him in the Musee Carnavalet. Remember when we were leaving and went through the exhibits on the revolution? He was there, in one of the paintings. His name is Maximilien Robespierre and, Ben, under his name the plaque read, LEADER OF THE FRENCH REVOLUTION."

"You're sure it was the same man?"

"Yes, I'm certain of it. I don't remember ever meeting or seeing him. Of course, many people are at Versailles daily, but I don't think we've ever been introduced."

"Robespierre..." Ben went over to the bookcase and reached for the now familiar history book. He located an entire chapter dedicated to the revolution, a chapter he had skipped over before. He immediately began poring over the facts. They were chilling. Robespierre was indeed a leader, and completely committed to the abolishment of the monarchy. He rallied for the deaths of Louis and Marie, and anyone else he thought were sympathizers of the king and queen. As Ben read on, he discovered that Robespierre dies nine months after Marie, ironically, by guillotine. Toward the end of the Reign of Terror, when hundreds of souls were guillotined daily, the citizens eventually turned not only on the aristocracy, but also on anyone in power. Robespierre was another casualty of a country gone mad.

Ben shook his head and handed the book to Marie, who quickly read the account. "According to the date of his birth he's three years younger than me. He looked so much older."

"What year did you say it was when you came forward?"

"1773."

Ben quickly calculated in his head. "He would only be 15 that year." They stared at one another, not understanding.

"Perhaps he came to this century when he was older," said Marie.

"I guess anything is possible."

"I wonder what he knows? I wonder if he's found out about my death or even about... his own?"

"I don't know, but he must be following you, watching you! There's no other explanation for you seeing him so many times. He's getting bolder too, more threatening. I don't like it. I don't like it at all."

Marie got up and paced the room. She was feeling agitated, fearful. She wanted these questions to end. She wanted to be free. She turned to Ben, "I hesitate to bring this up now, but I had a thought earlier. Something I think might help resolve things for me."

"Go on..."

"Walking home from the Conciergerie this morning, I had a strong urge to face more of my past, and somehow, possibly secure my future. I want to return to Versailles. That is where it all began. When I left there before, I was confused and upset, not thinking clearly. Maybe if I go back, I'll see something, maybe a clue to how I got here. Do you think we could go there, together? It might..."

"No! There is no reason to go there! I don't think it's safe for you mentally or physically to go back there. It will only make things worse!" Both were shocked at his outburst. She bowed her head, her eyes filling with tears. She felt her fragile world falling apart and ran to the bedroom closing the door behind her.

Ben didn't understand why, but he felt enormous jealousy as she discussed her desire to return to Versailles. Why wasn't he enough for her? He knew his thoughts weren't making any sense, but that didn't matter. He told himself she was right, maybe it was for the best, but where did common sense fit into this situation? He didn't like it. He wanted things to go on as they were before last night... before the nightmares... before the revelation of Robespierre.

Ben went out on the balcony and took a deep breath of the cold, crisp air. *Why did she go out without me this morning?* It wasn't that he wanted to keep her prisoner in the apartment, but when they first met, she needed him for everything, food, shelter, safety. She needed him to show her how things worked—simple things, like the oven, the faucet, the TV. Now, he realized, she did not need him in the same way as she did before. She was trying on her own to take charge. For the first time it occurred to him that she could choose to walk out of the apartment at any time and never come back.

I can't lose her... I just can't! He walked over to the bedroom and knocked lightly on the door. "Please, I need to be alone," was all she said. He waited a moment, and not hearing another sound, he walked over to the TV and turned it on. He would wait.

Half an hour later, Marie emerged from the bedroom. She gave Ben a weak smile. His eyes followed her as she walked over to the kitchen and made herself a cup of tea. She sat down on the couch next to him. "I've decided you're right. I don't need to go to Versailles. It will be too difficult for me. We'll just continue on, as before."

Ben felt relieved, but a tinge of guilt hit him as well. He knew he should be more supportive, but he didn't have it in him. He wanted her to find contentment and peace in the here and now.

"I think that's a good idea. But whatever we do, we must keep our eyes open for Robespierre. Don't worry, Marie, I will not let anything happen to you. For now, please don't leave the apartment without me. It's not safe."

"Yes… I need to be safe. I understand," she answered slowly, methodically.

They ate dinner and went to bed. Ben fell right to sleep, exhausted from staying up with Marie the night before, but his rest did not last. She continued having dreams, tossing, turning, and murmuring all through the night. He didn't understand what had changed. It was as if she was being drawn back to the past by an invisible force.

Early the next morning, sunlight streamed in the windows, awakening Ben. He turned over to check on Marie, but the other side of the bed was empty. *She must be making coffee*, he thought. His mind wandered. It was funny how just a few days ago, romance was the only thing on his mind. Now, all that had changed. Now he only wanted their relationship to survive whatever was happening to her. He lay there thinking about what might lie ahead. He finally got up and went into the bathroom to brush his teeth. He noticed her rosary dangling from the hook on the door where she placed it often.

He dressed for work and walked into the living area. Marie was sitting on the balcony writing in her journal. He opened the balcony door and sat down beside her. She did not acknowledge him at first. She finished writing, closed the journal, and without looking at him she spoke. "I'm better today. Although I did not sleep well, I'm all right. I've given much thought to my life and all that's happened, and you are right, I will try and live in the here and now completely."

"It's the only way. I feel sick when I think about what happens to you in the past. Considering everything, I think it would be foolish to take a chance of going back to Versailles. It's too risky." He hated to be morbid, but he felt he had to impress upon her the danger, the unknown.

"You're right." Immediately picking up her journal and pen, she got up.

Ben knew the conversation was over, but he didn't feel she was saying all she wanted to say. He glanced at his watch. It was past time to leave for work. "Let's continue this discussion when I get home. I'll be back around 3:00." He got up to leave, and touched her on the arm as he spoke. "Try to relax, and for today, try to put it all out of your mind." She nodded. He kissed the top of her head gently, turned, and left.

Chapter 22

The train began moving forward toward its destination. Marie sat back, leaned against the window and closed her eyes, wanting to shut out the world. She imagined she was in a golden carriage, dressed in all her finery, her hair done up in the latest fashion. She saw herself journeying through a dense forest, rather than past the hodgepodge of buildings and homes in the suburbs between Paris and Versailles. She was going back home. She was taking control of her life. Immediately, Ben's face flashed across her mind, and she began to argue with herself. *NO! I'm not leaving him. I'm taking one final look at my past. I must see if there's something I missed... a clue. I must know if the possibility to go back exists. Then, I will decide where I belong. I will take control of my destiny, my future.* She felt empowered. Being thrust into the 21st century had certainly affected her ability to make decisions.

Before she knew it, the train pulled into the station and Marie exited and began her walk to the palace. The cars speeding along the road no longer bothered her. She thought back to the day she hid in the bushes when she first walked out of the palace. She had adjusted to all the sights and sounds of this modern era.

However, the past continued to haunt her, and she constantly looked over her shoulder to make sure she wasn't being followed.

She turned a corner and there the palace stood in all its glory. She smiled. Despite everything, she was home. She passed through the massive gates and strode across the cobblestone courtyard. It was early afternoon. Not many people were in line to enter the palace; the bulk of them were already inside. Marie ignored the main entrance, and instead went left. She walked past several buildings and down a long flight of stairs on her way to the L'Orangerie.

She loved this area of the gardens. Usually it was full of tropical plants and flowers, but at this late time in the year, only the palm trees remained. Standing tall in green wooden boxes, they could easily be wheeled into the conservatory at night to protect them from the winter temperatures. She sat amongst the trees wistfully gazing out across the man-made lake and the boxwoods planted around her in perfect symmetry. The entire grounds of the chateau were designed to perfection, in perfect balance and harmony.

She would wait here in this open, peaceful setting. But she didn't feel peaceful, constantly scanning the distance for any signs of Robespierre. She planned to go inside right before closing and visit her bedroom one last time. If she had one more look and no clues were found, her decision would be final. She would leave her former home, her past, and return to Ben, forever.

* * *

Ben hurried home as soon as his shift was over. It had been a long day. He was anxious to get back and see how Marie was feeling.

Am I wrong about all this? Should we go back to Versailles to search for clues? The thought of it left him agitated and tense. He knew eventually things would come to a head; he just wasn't sure how.

Relieved to arrive at his building, he bounded up the stairs. He opened the apartment door and found the living area empty. He glanced over to the balcony and found it empty as well. Panic immediately seized him. He called out to Marie as he opened the bedroom door and didn't find her there either. The bathroom door was closed, and he felt momentary hope. He lightly knocked and called her name. No answer. He opened the door and his spirit fell. He frantically searched the apartment for a note, a sign, anything that might help him find out where she had gone, but in his heart, he knew. She had gone to Versailles, alone. *No, no, no!* He knew there was only one thing to do. He immediately ran for the door, his medical bag still slung over his shoulder.

He hurried through the streets like a madman to catch the metro to the train station. Once there, he paced back and forth. He had just missed the train and would have to wait 20 minutes for the next one. He looked back and forth across the station, hoping to catch a glimpse of her. Questions raged through his mind. *What if I'm wrong and she hasn't gone to Versailles after all?* He felt helpless, but this was the only thing he knew to do. He had to find her, protect her from Robespierre.

Ben finally boarded, and as the train left the station, he leaned back in his seat. In his imagination, he saw his entire relationship with Marie play out like a movie. He loved her. He loved her so much he ached. Her gentle spirit, her sweetness, her wonder at the new world as she explored it with him had captivated his heart. He thought back over the meals they had shared in the apartment and in the quiet cafés in his neighborhood. He remembered evenings spent in front of the fire and nights spent in the same bed. He imagined them being intimate. He had waited for what felt like an eternity—waited for her to be ready. Now, it might never happen.

His reverie was interrupted when he heard his stop announced. He exited the train and hurried through the streets of the town. He wished he knew what time she had left the apartment. It would help him immensely to know how much time had passed between their arrivals in Versailles. He followed the signs to the palace, and as he turned the last corner, there it was. He was taken aback at the enormity of it. He had always planned to come see the famous chateau, but had never made the short trip from Paris, always too busy to make time. Now he regretted his apathy. If he had been here before, he would at least have some knowledge of the layout.

Multiple buildings spread out in front of him like a miniature city. His task was immense. He walked through the gates, followed the signs, and finally stood in line with a few others at the main entrance. He declined the guided tour, instead buying a ticket to tour the palace on his own. The woman selling the tickets explained the advantages of getting the audio guide, but he declined. She eyed him suspiciously as he rocked back and forth on his heels, obviously in a great hurry. He turned to leave and ignored her as she called out to him that he had left his guide map behind.

Straightaway he began searching from room to room, following the general direction of the crowd. He took no time to enjoy the splendor all around him. He felt Marie's presence. Not in a way that meant she was around the next corner, but her essence, almost like her spirit was embedded in the walls. This overwhelming feeling only caused him to move faster and faster, scanning each room for a glimpse of her amongst the crowd. He never stopped to admire the masterpiece paintings, the ornate carvings, the woodwork, or the celestial scenes painted on the ceiling of every room.

With each area he searched, he got more and more discouraged. There was no sign of her. He had no idea where she could be. He could search for hours and never find her. Even more upsetting were the areas he passed that were blocked from the public. *She could be anywhere,* he thought wearily. *What if Robespierre is here? What if he finds her first?*

Finally, he exited out the back to the gardens. The sight took his breath away. The property went on for miles and miles, acre upon acre. It would be impossible to search it all. The sun was low, the shadows long. He knew the palace would close in a little over an hour. Aimlessly, he continued walking, searching, hoping.

Chapter 23

Marie paced back and forth in the garden as she waited for sunset, and for Versailles to empty out for the day. She wondered what Ben would think when he came home to an empty apartment. She felt terrible leaving the way she did, but she was compelled. *Maybe this trip was foolish,* she thought. Time seemed to move at an excruciatingly slow pace as the minutes ticked by. At one point she considered leaving, but no, she would see it through. She sat down on a stone bench, impeccably carved with gentle swirls and fleur-de-lis.

After what felt like an eternity, the sun began to set. *It won't be long now.* She closed her eyes a moment to gather her courage. Her stomach was churning, thinking of returning to her room—her past—one last time. Memories of waking up there, so alone, so frightened, were not memories she wanted to revisit. She finally stood up from the bench and turned. She gasped. Running toward her with a pained expression on his face was Ben, her Ben. Relief overcame her and her fear subsided. They fell into each other's arms, both apologizing. Happy tears flowed down Ben's face as he embraced her, never wanting to ever let go.

"I thought I would never see you again!"

"I'm sorry, so sorry. I felt I had to come. I knew you were against it, so I waited until you left for work."

"It's okay, it's okay. I understand. I'm not angry. I'm the one who is sorry... sorry I didn't respect your need to return. I'm just glad I found you."

"Me too."

They sat down on the bench and Marie leaned into Ben for comfort, his strong arms around her. She noticed his medical bag down by his feet. "Were you planning on saving me with that?"

Ben laughed. "No, I ran out of the apartment so fast after you, I didn't even realize I still had it with me."

As the sun finally dipped below the horizon, a cold wind whipped up out of nowhere. Distant thunder rolled through the sky and the air suddenly felt damp.

"What would you like to do now? Should we get going? Have you seen enough?"

"Actually, no. My plan was to visit my bedroom one last time."

"You haven't done that yet?"

"No, I was waiting until the palace cleared out."

"Do you want me to come with you?"

"Yes. Today has been miserable. I never want us to be apart again. Come with me. I'll show it to you. I just need a few moments and we'll catch the train back to Paris." Ben was relieved to hear her say that.

The wind grew colder and a light mist began to fall. The hour was late. All the other people had left the garden and gone inside except one. One lone figure stood listening, concealed behind a large statue standing guard at the edge of the garden.

Marie led Ben quickly up the massive steps to a back entrance of the palace, through a door hidden from view. As they walked from room to room, she felt calm, holding Ben's hand as they went, sharing some of her memories with him, although not stopping to reminisce. She knew their time was short, the palace would be closing shortly.

She opened a side door expertly built into the wall, and Ben followed her through it. They crept silently up and down empty hallways and staircases. Untold treasures were hidden in this secret space. In one of the larger rooms, huge sheets covered furniture, paintings, sculptures, and other relics from the past. These items were preserved, stored in dark rooms, under cover, until time to pull them out for a special exhibition or event. Under different circumstances, they would have paused and taken a closer look, but not tonight.

Marie led Ben down a short flight of stairs, and as they rounded the corner, there it was, her bedroom. Fortunately, they were alone. Most of the palace had cleared out due to the nasty weather. Only a few minutes remained until Versailles closed for the day. Ben and Marie stood together at the golden ornate railing in front of the large bed she and Louis had shared. It was exactly as it had been when she woke up in the future just a short time ago. She gazed around the room trying to uncover any clues as to what had happened. There were none.

She turned to Ben, removed her rosary from around her neck, and placed it in his hand closing his fingers around it. Looking into his eyes she said, "I'm ready to move forward. I want you to have this rosary, my sole possession, as a token of my love for you, a symbol that I'm ready to leave the past behind."

Ben was overcome, unable to speak, and she turned for one last look at the room. Feeling she needed a moment of privacy, he put the rosary around his neck, threw his bag over his shoulder and walked over to look out the large set of windows. Not only did the mist continue to fall, but a thick fog had rolled in as well. He thought about how far they had come. He waited, knowing she was saying goodbye forever to her former life.

Marie was ready to move on, but not before she stood still and remembered being a scared young girl, arriving at Versailles all those years ago. She remembered spending her first night in this room. Alone. No family or friends anywhere around to comfort her, or to tell her everything would be all right. She thought about her wedding day, surrounded by strangers. She realized how brave she had been, how strong. Then she shuddered once more thinking about what might have been.

Folding her arms against the chill, she turned to leave, but a slight movement of the heavy fabric hanging down from the bed canopy caught her eye. She stepped forward, craning her neck to see what was there, and without warning, a man leapt out, grabbed her, and covering her mouth with his hand he began dragging her across the room. Ben heard the commotion, dashed across the room and jumped on the man's back, which freed Marie as both men crashed to the ground.

"RUN!" yelled Ben, as he tussled with the stranger. Immediately she ran to the nearest door, the one to her dressing room just to the side of the bed. She disappeared through the doorway, and seconds later the man broke free and ran after her. Just before he reached the door, Ben tackled him, and the two men fell through the doorway together.

Instantly, they were in complete darkness.

Part 2

Chapter 24

Marie felt an odd sensation that her body was still in motion, and yet she lay still, frozen to the floor. Every muscle in her body ached. She cautiously wiggled her fingers and toes, and as her mind cleared, quickly rose to her feet, weaving back and forth for a moment, "Ben? Ben, where are you?"

As her eyes adjusted to the dim light, panic swept through her body. Everything had returned to the way it was just two weeks ago. Her combs and brushes, jewelry and clothes were all back in their rightful places. *No, no, not now!* With trepidation she entered the bedroom. There she found her desk angled across one corner of the room and her golden harp standing vigil in the opposite corner. Her favorite music box was back on the side table next to the bed. Devastated, she whispered, "Ben, are you here?" Silence. She spun in circles searching the room. The candlelight flickered across the walls distorting her shadow like a bad omen. She was back—back in the 1700's. A wave of despair came over her like a shroud. She had come back... without him.

Walking over to the mirror, she studied her reflection. She looked the same, but felt oh so different. Suddenly, she heard someone approaching. "Ben, is that you?" she called. She watched expectantly as the golden door handle across the room slowly turned.

Her hopes were dashed when a guardsman entered the room as he always did on his nightly check. He gasped, "Mon Dieu! Madame Antoinette! You are here! Are you well? I must report your presence to the dauphin at once!"

"What do you mean?" asked Marie.

"Your whereabouts, Madame, have been unknown for weeks. The search has been unending. The entire palace has been turned upside down, as well as the grounds. We had all but given up hope."

Marie was dumbfounded. Another guard came into the room and upon seeing her, immediately turned and ran out yelling, "The dauphine has been located! The dauphine has been located!"

How would she ever explain?

Chapter 25

Ben opened his eyes and stared into the darkness. He slowly rolled over and pushed himself up on his knees, his head throbbing with a pain so intense he almost blacked out. Disoriented, he took a deep breath, and with all the strength he could muster, stood to his feet. "Marie, where are you?" He called to her over and over, as he groped in the darkness like a blind man trying to feel his way through unfamiliar territory. The silence was devastating. *Where is she?* He knew he had seen her run into this very room just moments ago. He took a few steps forward, his knees buckled, and he fell to the ground unconscious.

In another part of the palace, Robespierre continued to drag himself along; his leg wound had split open and was oozing blood. When Ben had tackled him, they crashed onto the wood floor on the other side of the door as if they had fallen from a great distance. Robespierre was in fight mode immediately, but Ben lay crumpled next to him, motionless. He nudged him and then shook his shoulder. Nothing. *He must be dead.*

Unable to support his weight on the injured leg, he began crawling and dragging his body forward through the halls. His leg hadn't healed properly from the original injury and he was losing blood fast. He knew he needed help. Sweat seeped from his forehead and his elbows ached as he used them to move his body. It was slow going. If he could make his way out of the palace, maybe he could find assistance.

* * *

Ben opened his eyes, staring sideways across the room from his horizontal position on the floor. As his eyes adjusted to the bright moonlight streaming in through the windows, something dark crossed his line of sight inches from his face. Instinctively he jerked his head back, just as a rat slowly crawled by as if Ben didn't exist. The sight sickened him, and he stood up quickly to gain a feeling of control over his surroundings. His thoughts turned to the man that had grabbed Marie, the man Ben was fighting just before they fell through the door together. *Could it have been Robespierre?*

He reached his hand up and felt a large knot near his temple. He cautiously moved through the doorway, stepping back into Marie's bedchamber. Incredibly, it had been completely destroyed. The heavy ornate chandelier that had been hanging over the bed was in a million pieces on the floor. The bedclothes were torn, the mattress slashed to bits, and trash littered the room everywhere he looked. The air was stuffy and had an odd, overwhelming odor, almost more than he could bear. He called again for Marie, but there was no answer. It was as if she disappeared into thin air.

His fear began to mount as he searched from room to room, only to find more destruction and no sign of Marie. As he made his way further into the palace, he noticed a red substance smeared on the floor. He knelt down to confirm his suspicion. *It's blood! I must hurry. Maybe she is hurt, lying somewhere needing help.* Then another thought came to him, *What if the man has her?* He hurried along the corridors covertly, not knowing what he might find.

He came to a large open room and was shocked to see a woman dressed in rags and a filthy child sitting silently on the floor in front of a fireplace. "Excuse me. Have you seen a young woman come by?" asked Ben. The woman turned to him, the deep lines on her face telling a story of sadness and hardship. She looked into his eyes for just a moment, then slowly turned back to the fire in silence. The child never moved. "Ma'am, please, have you seen a young woman, or a man pass this way?" The woman never looked up. He did not feel threatened by the pair, only pity. It was obvious they had taken up residence in the abandoned, desolate chateau and would be no help to him.

Ben noticed a candlestick tossed carelessly on the floor. He picked it up, and searched until he found a taper. Avoiding eye contact with the woman, he walked over to the fire, bent down, and lit his candle. Now he had better light for his search. As he left the room, he shook off the eerie feeling the miserable pair gave him. They looked like ghosts, illuminated only by the dancing flames of the fire.

The candle flickered as he walked on. Moments later, he heard a faint sound in the distance. He rushed toward it and rounding the next corner, he saw a man dragging himself along the black and white tile floor. Immediately Ben recognized him. "What have you done with Marie?" The man glanced back and began moving as fast as he possibly could, but within seconds Ben towered over him. He moved the candle down to see the man's face, and noticed the bloody leg. His medical training kicked in. "You need help. Tell me what you've done with Marie, and I'll examine your leg."

"I don't know where she is," he sneered.

"That's impossible. She was right there, with both of us."

"Once you and I hit the ground, you did not move. I thought you were dead. She was nowhere to be found."

"You're lying. Tell me where she is!"

"I told you, I don't know."

"What about the palace, the sudden destruction. What do you make of it?"

"Don't you understand?" he said knowingly. "We are not in your time anymore, we've come back to mine."

Ben felt terror move through his body in a sickening wave. His stomach dropped, "What do you mean? That's impossible. It can't be true!"

"But it is true. This is the condition Versailles was in when I first stepped through her dressing room door two weeks ago. Now I know. That door is the path to the future, but also back to the present."

Ben sat down on the floor completely devastated by the news that he was now in the 18th century... but how could he be sure? Not knowing whether he could trust the man's word or not, he asked, "Is your name Robespierre?"

"Yes... Maximilien Robespierre. How did you know?"

"Marie recognized you from a painting in a museum." Ben decided to gather as much information as possible. "I'm curious, how did you survive in my time?"

"I managed."

"But how?"

"I slept down by the Seine, stealing food, clothing—whatever it took to survive. When I arrived in the future, I was immediately chased out of Versailles. I ran out of the palace and hid close by. The following day, I saw Madame Antoinette behind the palace gates, which were locked. She looked so young, so different... but I recognized her immediately. I slept in the park and the next day I followed her to the train station, to Paris, and finally to your dwelling."

"But why?"

"She was my only link to the past. I thought she might know what had happened, but it became clear she was as lost as I was."

They sat in silence, each sizing the other up. Ben would not forget that Robespierre had tried to harm Marie and would try again if he got the chance. He also had no idea what had transpired while he lay unconscious in Marie's dressing room. Ben decided an alliance was necessary with Robespierre, in case he was hiding information about her whereabouts. He noticed the blood pooling under his leg and said, "Let me to examine your leg."

"Why? What can you do about it?"

"I'm a trained medical technician." Ben sat the candle on the ground, grabbed the bottom of the pant leg and ripped it up the seam. He found a deep cut in the thigh area beginning to show signs of infection. "I must tend to this immediately, or you'll eventually lose your leg." Ben remembered the medical backpack he had with him when he fell through the door. "Stay here. I'll be right back."

With that Ben made his way back to Marie's dressing room, found his bag, and quickly returned. Kneeling down and searching through his kit, he was thankful for the extensive medical supplies he had with him. "My name is Ben," he said, as he gathered what he needed. "This is going to be painful." Ben poured antiseptic over the wound. Robespierre shrieked in pain and scooted away awkwardly.

"What are you doing?" he asked, seething in anger.

"Cleansing the wound."

"Let me be!"

"No. If I don't take care of it, you will lose your leg, or worse, die of gangrene."

Ben numbed the area before suturing it, administered a shot of Penicillin, and then wrapped the leg up in clean gauze. Robespierre was relieved when Ben finished. "It should feel better in a day or two, but you must stay off it," said Ben.

"You expect me to stay here, in this place, full of filth and rats?"

"If you wish to get better, yes. If you reopen the wound, it may never heal."

Robespierre realized his precarious position and it angered him. Looking into Ben's eyes with hatred he spoke, "You know this changes nothing. She will still lose her head." Then pausing for dramatic effect, he said, "If she hasn't already."

"What do you mean?"

"I know the outcome. I saw the plaque embedded in the square. If it hasn't already happened, I will see that it does."

Ben's blood ran cold. *If it hasn't already happened? What does he mean? Could I already be too late? If not, I just saved the life of the man bent on Marie's destruction.* Ben looked at Robespierre in disgust, grabbed his backpack, turned and walked away. All he could think was, *I must find her before he does.*

As soon as Ben left, Robespierre's mind started racing. *Where is that vile Marie Antoinette? I must find her. The last time I walked through this palace, she was in prison in the Tuileries with the king and her children. I must get to Paris as soon as possible and see if she's still alive.*

Despite Ben's warning, Robespierre stood up slowly. The bleeding had stopped. He took a few shaky steps. They were slow but steady, so he limped along, leaving the palace through a back exit. He planned to go into town, find out the date, and speak to a few of his friends. If she is still alive, he will return to Paris immediately. He was completely devoted to the fall of the monarchy and was determined to see it through to the end. He felt the only way for the new republic to survive, and for the Declaration of the Rights of Man and of the Citizen to be permanently established, was for the king and queen to be removed from the citizen's lives forever in a public display. Exile would not do.

As for what had happened to him over the past two weeks, he didn't understand, and knew no one would believe it anyway. He was relieved to be back in his time. It was a secret he would keep until his tasks were complete. In the meantime, he would pen a letter to his trusted friend, Jean Baptiste Delambre, the well-known mathematician and astronomer. Maybe his friend could make sense of what happened. They could be on the cusp of the most important discoveries in history... but not until Louis and Marie were dead. Only then would the Republic live on and, most importantly, with his new-found knowledge of the future, Robespierre would be in a position of great power. The world and its future would be his.

Chapter 26

1773

Once the guardsmen left her room, Marie scrambled. Being thrown back into her life so abruptly, she reacted without any time to think, or plan what she would say. She dashed back into her dressing room and changed into a robe quickly, stuffing her modern clothing into a blue silk box and hiding it in the top of one of her many closets. She slipped her tiny feet into a pair of crystal-incrusted slippers, returned to her room, and stretched out on a red velvet chaise lounge. At the last second, she reached over, grabbed a book, and opened it to a random page. She slowed her breathing and acted as if it was a day like any other.

Moments later, Louis raced into the room along with other members of the court. He stared at her in disbelief. He knelt by the chaise lounge and took her hand, "Marie, is it really you? We had given you up for dead. Are you all right?"

"Why yes, Louis, I'm fine."

Puzzled by her attitude, he stood up. His tone immediately changed. "Where have you been?" he demanded.

"I've... I've been away."

"What do you mean... away?"

Marie remained silent, her mind racing.

"Marie? Tell me, where have you been?" Louis waited. The others stood by, silently.

The words suddenly tumbled out of her mouth. "One day I was feeling particularly suffocated by the constant presence of the court all around me." She deliberately paused as she looked into the faces of those around the room. "I went for a long walk in the gardens and ended up at the Petite Trianon. I knew the king's mistress was gone on a trip, so I went inside. The place was empty, so... I stayed. I knew no one would look for me there."

"You were there, all this time? That is preposterous! How could you do such a thing? Right here under our noses, while we combed the palace and the grounds?" Louis paused and eyed her suspiciously. "What did you eat? There is no food or drink stored out there when no one is in residence."

Marie's face went white. She could feel the awkwardness in the room with all eyes upon her. Her closest friend and confidant, Princess de Lamballe stepped forward. "Please forgive me, but I helped Madame. I was with her on the walk, so I knew of her plan and desire to be alone. I took meals to her each day. I am so sorry, I beg your forgiveness." She bowed her head.

Marie's eyes met Princess de Lamballe's for just an instant. "Please Louis, don't be angry. She did not plan to deceive anyone. I swore her to secrecy." Marie knew she sounded like a spoiled child, wanting her way no matter who she hurt, but she had to make Louis believe her, at least for now.

Averse to confrontation, Louis looked self-consciously around the room while the others waited for his reaction. Finally, he nodded his head slowly. "I see. You desired some privacy. It's well understood, but the way you went about it is improper. You must never disappear like that again. I must be informed. Understand my dear?"

"Of course, Louis. I am sorry if my behavior disturbed you." With that, the subject was closed.

The other courtiers eyed one another in disgust and before the sun rose the next morning, gossip and rumors had traveled throughout the court and beyond. Outlandish lies were spread about what Marie was doing at the Trianon during her absence. It was just the kind of thing those envious of her position needed. Ugly rumors of affairs with stable boys and other private liaisons persisted. Even tales of intimate relationships with her ladies-in-waiting and Princess de Lamballe were rampant. Marie, often referred to as "The Austrian," was hated all the more as time went on. This was the beginning of her downfall.

Chapter 27

Ben left through the ornate golden gates to see if Marie had made her way outside to look for him. She would be upset, alone, and confused as he was. His heart ached. Right at the moment their relationship was flourishing, disaster happened. He had let her down. He would never forgive himself, but how could he have known they would be transported to the past, a past that held certain death for her? He didn't see a hint of Marie. The guilt was overwhelming.

It was late, perhaps around midnight. Ben made his way into the center of town and saw a faint light up ahead. As he got closer, he realized it was coming from a small tavern. Hearing voices, he peered in through the iron grate built into a crudely hewn wooden door. The room was small. At this late hour, only two men sat at one of the tiny square tables scattered about. They were deep in conversation. Ben steeled himself and walked through the door.

The room was hot and smelled of stale beer and other odors he could not place. The smoke from the stove, the candles, and lanterns burned his eyes. He took a seat on a stool at the bar, getting odd looks from the two men. Not only was he a stranger, he was unusually dressed. Eyeing him, they paused their conversation mid-sentence. Ben prayed they would not address him. Finally, they turned and went back to their banter. He listened carefully.

"How long do you think they will keep the king and queen locked up like common criminals?"

"Not long enough if you ask me!"

"They can't sit in the Tuileries forever."

"Sure they can! They can rot in there for all I care. They need to suffer as we citizens have suffered. All those years, gardening at Versailles, for what? First a peasant's wage, and finally no payment at all, while little Miss Antoinette built herself an empire."

"I agree. We were cheated for sure, but what about the beheadings? Things seem to be getting out of control, especially in Paris. Is the new authority any better?"

"You better watch what you say. There are ears everywhere." They both glanced over at Ben. The older of the two lowered his voice, "No matter." The man laughed and said, "You certainly wouldn't pass for a nobleman or a lord, so you're safe." He took a big swig of his beer and made a gesture with his hand across his neck.

The other man shook his head. "I don't know. Times are uncertain. At least with King Louis, we had peace." They continued drinking their beer in silence, deep in thought.

Once the men began discussing this year's pitiful crops due to lack of rain, Ben turned and spoke to the barkeeper. "Sir, could you spare a cup of water?"

"You aren't from around here, are you?" the burly barkeeper spat out, as he slid a tin cup towards Ben.

"No, just passing through." Ben tried to act nonchalant, but as he brought the cup to his mouth, he realized immediately he shouldn't drink it, regardless of his burning thirst. "Could you point me to the road to Paris?"

"Walk down to the corner and take the first road to the right."

"Thank you." He got off the stool and turned to leave, and there, hanging on a nail right next to the door was a grimy calendar, so yellowed by the constant presence of smoke he could hardly read it. But there it was, the answer to the question that nagged him... the month, June, the year, 1791.

Trembling, Ben left the tavern, his mind churning with times, dates, years. He couldn't keep it all straight. He was shocked, yet thankful to hear that Marie was in prison at the Tuileries, instead of the alternative. He still had time. *But how did she get from Versailles to the Tuileries? When? Did she come back in time to a different year than me?* The disdain the old man at the tavern had for Marie was shocking. Ben knew one thing for certain; he must get to Paris, and quickly.

The journey was long and slow. He had a lot of time to reflect about the past, which was now the present. *If it's now 1791, Marie will be in her 30's. Will she even know me?* There was also the constant nagging question of Robespierre and his whereabouts. He had three major advantages, money, connections, and a position of power. Ben had nothing—nothing but his love for Marie. Each time he thought of the end of the story, he quickened his steps. He must reach her first.

He traveled as fast as his feet would carry him. He stopped to rest only when exhaustion took over. Once during the night, he heard a horse and rider coming down the path. He hid behind some bushes and watched from a safe distance. The rider passed by so quickly he couldn't be sure if it was Robespierre or not. Thankfully, he heard rushing water, and quickly located a stream just beyond the trees. Kneeling at the bank, he cupped his hands and drank the water until his thirst was quenched. He then continued walking, one step at a time, thinking only of the moment he would see Marie. He vowed to never let her out of his sight again.

Chapter 28

1773

Marie withdrew to bed early that evening, her mind whirling with thoughts of Ben. She repeatedly went back and forth through the doorway to her dressing room, testing it, just in case, but time stood still.

When Louis came to bed later, he was distant—not that he had ever approached her in any kind of romantic way. In the years since their wedding day, they had been cordial to one another, and usually had pleasant conversation. Louis was kind and generous to her, but that's as far as it went, despite her occasional advances towards him. Tonight, he was obviously still upset about her disappearance. She decided to broach the subject cautiously to gauge his reaction.

"Louis, I want to ask you something."

"Yes?"

"Do you believe it's possible to travel through time?"

Louis raised his eyebrows, "What do you mean?"

"I'm not sure, I was just wondering if you thought it was possible. Do you think a person could travel to another time period?"

"No, I don't. I read about the theory in a book a while ago, but it is considered more of a fantasy than a real possibility. I don't see how it would be achieved." Louis paused and studied her face. "Marie, what disturbs you? First the disappearance, and now this talk of traveling to another time. Are you unhappy here at Versailles?"

Marie quickly changed the tone of their conversation. "Oh no, Louis, I'm very happy here." She smiled lovingly and continued. "I let my imagination run away with me I suppose. I apologize... and again Louis, I'm sorry about worrying everyone with my disappearance. I wanted some time to myself, but it was quite foolish of me."

"Just see that it doesn't happen again. Goodnight." With that Louis turned over to go to sleep. Their conversation was over.

Marie tossed and turned. She knew what had happened to her was real. She knew she had gone forward two hundred years and met Ben. She had experienced a life quite different from the one she had now. Wondering if she would ever make sense of it she finally rolled over and fell into a fitful sleep.

Days passed. Marie hardly ate, and when she did appear for meals, she seemed lost in a world of her own. She did what was expected of her, as well as she could. In her daily walks through the gardens, she often had a faraway look in her eyes and those around her kept a constant watch on her behavior.

Overwhelmed with longing for Ben, it no longer bothered her that Louis was inattentive in the bedroom. She knew she had to produce an heir, but it no longer seemed important. In fact, she was glad she remained a virgin and even had thoughts of saving herself for Ben, should they ever meet again. She often sat on the velvet chaise lounge, gazing at the doorway to her dressing room, longing for Ben to step through.

Months went by. The court was abuzz with talk of Marie's disappearance and her strange behavior. Some thought she was losing her mind. Others were content to continue the gossip, making stories up as they went along. One thing was certain, there was no doubt in anyone's mind that she was a blot on France. Surely, she alone was the reason she and Louis remained childless.

Marie remembered all she had read about her future, but it seemed so far away, so distant, that she refused to think about it. She was living her life as if Ben would come back for her and save her from it all. What Marie didn't realize was that the tide had already turned. The lies being planted about her now would persist for years and would eventually add fuel to the hatred toward the royals and all those associated with them. Close confidants tried to help, begging her to start appearing at court functions again, telling her it was dangerous to be absent. They suggested strongly that she should answer the rumors, or try to counteract them in some way to defend herself. She ignored their pleas as she sat by the window, day after day, staring out at the grounds of Versailles.

One afternoon Marie was so despondent, Louis called for one of the court's doctors and spoke to him about her unusual behavior and asked if he could help in some way. The doctor asked Marie extensive questions and observed her closely for a few days, and in the end, he told Louis he thought she was slowly going mad.

Louis refused to accept the doctor's diagnosis and immediately sent for the chief apothecary to discuss Marie's situation. After much observation, the apothecary and his assistants went right to work, concocting a mixture of poppy syrup, flower waters, and essences. They experimented with chemicals as well, even though mixing these substances together was in its infant stage in pharmaceutical science. When they felt certain they had produced something suitable to help the dauphine, they delivered it to Louis in a blue and white earthenware container along with a glass vile. "Measure out one vile in the morning and another in the evening. If she drinks this, we are confident she will be back to herself very soon."

Unfortunately, the amalgam had a damaging effect. By the second dose, Marie was hallucinating wildly, thrashing about in her bed, near hysterics. Thinking this was part of the cure, they continued with the doses each morning and evening. She was plagued with nightmares, fears, and anxieties.

The third night was especially difficult. It finally got so dreadful that Louis demanded the medicine be stopped. He was frightened and realized, perhaps for the first time, how much he cared for her. He kept a constant vigil by her bedside through the night.

In the early morning hours just before sunrise, Marie sat straight up in bed. Louis grabbed her hand. It was burning hot. Her mind spinning out of control, she jumped up and ran to her dressing room, feeling compelled to find the blue silk box she had hidden in a closet on her first night back. She mumbled over and over that she had to find it, feeling it held something crucial to her existence, but unable to remember what. She rummaged frantically through the closets, throwing clothes, shoes, bags, and jewelry everywhere in search of the box.

Louis, along with two of her servants watched in shock, not knowing how to stop this outburst. Finally, Marie turned to them with a wild look in her eyes. "My blue silk box, where is it?" The maids looked at one another questioningly. "You took it, you stole it," Marie screamed. The maids stepped back in horror. Louis grabbed Marie and hugged her tight, trying to calm her down.

"We will find it Marie, don't worry. Come back to bed."

"I can't... I won't!" Marie ran to her other closets and ransacked them looking for the box. Closet after closet she searched wildly. Finally, exhausted, she stopped. She had no idea why she felt compelled to find the box, but she did, and not finding it was devastating.

Louis led her back to bed and she quieted down. As the maids left the room, he assured them they were not suspects. It was obvious to Louis that Marie was either having a severe reaction to the medicine, or a complete mental breakdown. Worse, no one knew how to help her.

The residual effects of the concoction were long lasting. When she finally sat back up, she took tiny sips of water but no food. She slept for two days, and when she finally woke Lois was right there by her side. "My dear, how are you feeling?"

"I'm... not sure. What happened? How long have I been in bed?"

"Two days."

Marie was shocked. She took a few steps from the bed. Oddly, she felt rejuvenated for the first time in months. The cobwebs had cleared, however, memories of what had transpired over the past few days had vanished. Her memories of time travel and Ben were gone too—completely gone.

Despite feeling better, there were constant nagging thoughts in her head that were vague, just out of reach. As she continued to fully recover, those around her were forbidden to bring up any of the disturbing events. Louis treated her with extra care over the next months, and over time, she began to return to her old self.

What no one knew, not even her, was she now possessed a divided mind, and just beyond the imaginary partition, was a minefield of memories.

Chapter 29
Time Marches On

1774–1788

A year passed. Marie seemed much better. Louis was sure she had made a full recovery. She was living as she had before the "incident" as if it never happened. Her memories were locked away, but occasionally she would have flashes of déjà vu, which were fleeting and unsettling. When these feelings occurred, she froze, trying to reach out and grab the moment, to understand where it came from, but it always slipped away like a whiff of smoke.

Louis went back to his frequent hunts and to his favorite pastime, spending hours in his workshop fashioning metal locks and keys. Life was easy, other than the pressure that they produce an heir. Louis knew the problem was his and his alone, but he didn't have any idea how to overcome it.

On a beautiful day in May, Louis was out with his hunting party enjoying the lovely French countryside. When they stopped to rest their horses, they saw a rider in the distance closing in at great speed. He pulled his horse to an abrupt stop.

"Your grandfather, the king, is ill. You must come at once!" the rider announced, gasping for breath.

Just a few days later, Louis XV died of smallpox. As the bells rang out in the palace and in the towns throughout France, Louis and Marie's eyes met. In an instant, their lives changed... forever.

Louis was crowned King Louis XVI and celebrations broke out all over the land. Marie stood by his side as queen, always in silent support. Everyone knew 20-year-old Louis did not possess the self-confidence or experience to be an effective leader. He was quiet and introspective, easily swayed by his advisers who were often self-serving, not having France's best interest at heart.

Life went on for the new king and queen, and so did life at Versailles. Now the demand to produce an heir was paramount. Marie did all she could to entice Louis, but to no avail. She became bored with the sameness of life and the empty arms that longed to cradle a baby. Without children, or even the hope of a child to fill her days, she turned to other interests.

Fashion became her obsession. One of her favorite pastimes was choosing fabrics and patterns with the top clothing designers from Paris that visited her frequently. She created a dress book, full of swatches and drawings, a special place for her to keep track of her ever-expanding wardrobe. Not only were dresses a favorite of Marie's, but so were the signature hairstyles she wore to parties, balls, and official events. She employed a flamboyant hairdresser who would conspire with her to create outlandish hairstyles that were shocking, yet fabulous. Each time she debuted a new look, the style would be copied all over Europe. Maintaining her extensive wardrobe, shoes, jewelry, and hair came at great expense.

Marie had her small circle of close friends and confidants with whom she spent many hours a day, but she longed for excitement and begged Louis to take her places away from the palace. Even though Louis preferred the familiar surroundings of his home, he occasionally relented. Once while attending a masked ball at the Opera House in Paris, they met a young Swedish Officer, Count Axel de Ferson. Marie and Louis were quite impressed with the dashing young military officer, and they invited him to visit Versailles. He soon came, only staying a few days, but it was enough time for him to become completely enamored with the young queen. He vowed to come back and visit again.

Versailles evenings were spent in the salon, where the king and queen hosted elaborate late-night dinners where social and political business was conducted. After dinner, guests would retire to other rooms for games, music and dancing. Soon a new pastime evolved for Marie: gambling. Whether it was cards or dice, she sometimes played into the wee hours of the morning, well after Louis went to bed. He disapproved of her wasteful losses, but not wanting to upset her, he chose to ignore it.

Marie continued to receive letters from her mother, always reminding her of her "duty" to produce an heir, repeatedly reminding her that her place in France was not secure until a baby was born. Finally, Marie's brother, Joseph, was sent from Austria to Versailles to counsel with Louis. Whatever the conversation was, it did the trick. Finally, seven years after their wedding, they consummated their marriage. A year later, on December 19, 1778, Marie gave birth to a daughter, Marie Thérèse Charlotte. Although a male was preferred, Marie and Louis were ecstatic and would go on to have three more children: two boys and a girl.

Becoming a mother certainly mellowed Marie and many of her immature pastimes were forgotten. As fulfilling as motherhood was for her, ironically, she still felt an overwhelming sense of loneliness. She and Louis were close, but they never connected in the way Marie longed for. She often felt there was a missing piece, true happiness always eluding her. No one else could imagine that a woman with so much could still have secret desires, but she did. Somewhere deep in her heart, she knew there should be more. She also knew Louis was not capable of giving the kind of love she instinctively desired and somehow knew existed.

Nothing in her life was working out as she had imagined it as a young girl. The extravagances of Versailles were certainly appreciated, but deep down, she longed for a simpler, less formal life. She came up with an idea, a project that would become her crown jewel.

In the countryside just beyond the Petit Trianon, but still on the palace grounds, she began designing a tiny hamlet, a retreat for her and the children to go and have a semblance of a normal life. The imaginary village was built around a small lake and included a dairy, a mill, a house, as well as other buildings and gardens. Many afternoons they enjoyed playing with the animals, picking flowers, or floating around the tiny lake in a small rowboat. This miniature town became a favorite escape for her and her children, but as with many other things in Marie's life, it came at an extravagant price.

Spending so much time at the tiny hamlet, she was removed from the goings on at Versailles and ignorant of the feelings the French citizens had towards her. Talk of the revolution had begun. The citizens were disgusted at the wasteful spending of the king and queen, as they paid higher and higher taxes, while starving and begging for bread.

France had become a divided country, separated into three distinct groups: the nobility (the crown and those at court receiving privileges), the clergy (the religious faction), and the Third Estate (the commoners). With the country facing complete financial disaster due to wars, spending, and the overgenerous support of the American Revolution, it was time to ask the nobility and the clergy to give up some of their titles and privileges, and for the first time, to begin paying taxes. There was no other choice. The coffers were empty.

The Assembly of Notables gathered, each of the three groups having one vote. Louis' finance minister made a plea for the clergy and the nobility to realize that the only way out of financial ruin was to vote away their privileges and to begin paying taxes. The debate was lively. A vote was taken and, as always, the clergy and the nobility voted together, once again leaving the commoners out in the cold.

Louis was in a no-win situation, but incredibly, in the end, the bulk of the blame was set at Marie Antoinette's feet. The rumors of long ago were circulated again and again, each time growing in intensity and hatred. New rumors were formed and spread quickly. Obscene pamphlets were regularly distributed throughout Paris with Marie's image front and center. The uglier the rumors, the more they were believed. Marie was encouraged by her advisers to demand the punishment of the pamphleteers, but she refused. Marie never wanted anyone punished on her behalf. In the end it didn't matter, the people of France had turned against her, and the monarchy, for good.

Chapter 30
The Arrest

1789

Times were changing politically. For Marie, they were changing personally as well. Her world began spinning out of control. In June 1789, tragedy struck. Marie and Louis lost their first-born son, Louis Joseph, to tuberculosis at the age of seven. They were shattered, having already lost their youngest daughter, Sophie, just the year before. Louis Joseph had always been a frail child and they both felt the loss profoundly.

Marie and Louis barely had time to grieve. In July, the Bastille Prison in Paris was stormed in a rebel uprising. The king's guard's heads were slashed from their bodies, prisoners were set free, and the structure was set on fire. What had been feared for many months had become a reality just miles away. The revolution had begun.

The political unrest lasted for months. One evening, still despondent over the loss of Louis Joseph, Marie lay in bed, weeping. She was called to dinner. As she rose from her bed to ready herself, she heard voices echoing in the distance.

It sounds like chanting. Marie couldn't be sure, but as the minutes ticked by, the chanting became louder and louder. Suddenly two court guards came charging into her room. "Madame, a mob approaches. We fear they are after you and your family. Come with us immediately."

The mob was now in the courtyard and it was feared the palace would be overrun. Hands shaking, Marie grabbed her children from the next room and ran through a secret passageway to Louis' private apartments.

"Louis, we must leave at once!"

"Of course, Marie, but you and the children need immediate safety. The palace guards will protect you here. We will leave when the crowd disperses."

Marie stood, trembling with fear and clinging desperately to her two children. Piercing screams filled the air. The guards stationed at the entrance to the palace were being killed one by one. When the crowd called for the queen's head, Marie had never felt such terror in her entire life. Louis stood in silence, not sure what to do. Seeing his indecision, she gathered her courage and decided to address the crowd forthright. She had ignored almost all of the accusations hurled at her over the years, but now she would not shrink back. She would face her accusers and ask for mercy.

Marie trembled with trepidation as she opened the balcony doors overlooking the courtyard. She approached the railing, and her eyes swept over the crowd. Below her, in the beautiful courtyard of Versailles was an incensed mob, full of women hurling unspeakable insults at her, waving their pitchforks and torches in the air. *Perhaps,* she thought, *I can appeal to them as a mother*. Turning to ask for her children to join her on the balcony, her stomach lurched. Up on the top of one of the pikes was the head of a palace guard. She knew at that moment all sense of decency was lost. Not wanting to expose her children to such atrocities, she decided to remain on the balcony alone.

She quietly bowed to the crowd, knowing she was at their mercy. They fell silent. The torches glowed eerily in the night casting macabre shadows as the crowd stared up at her. Taken aback by her gesture, they stood silent for a few moments, gazing up at their queen. It only took one in the crowd to incite them back into a full riot. When the chanting began again, Marie turned and went back inside, shutting the balcony doors behind her.

Within moments, the crowd stormed the palace, breaking through windows and doors, destroying everything in their path. The scene was grisly as more guards lost their heads. The royal family was placed under house arrest, and told by a representative of the movement, that if they wished to live, they must travel to Paris under escort and face their opponents. Louis refused at first, but with no other option presented, he finally relented.

It took most of the night for the servants to pack up some of the royal belongings and load the numerous bags and trunks onto the opulent coaches and carriages. The four members of the royal family gathered into their private carriage, and as the sun rose, they made their way slowly to Paris escorted by the armed guards of the Republic. Louis and Marie felt unable to stop the current chain of events and did not realize they would never again return to Versailles. That day, the royal family was put under house arrest in the dismal, unkempt Tuileries Palace, where they would remain for the next 2 years. This move signaled the end of the ancient regime. The aristocratic, monarchic, political, and social system that had been in place in France for over 300 years was over.

Chapter 31

1791

The sun was just on the horizon when Ben approached Paris. The sight that met him was unimaginable. He had read about the living conditions of this general time period, but to experience it in person was more than he could endure. As he entered the city, the stench was overwhelming. He wanted to turn back, but knew he could not. He had to find Marie.

In the early morning light, he came upon a house with men's clothing hanging on a line in the yard. Seeing no one, he took the clothes and changed into them behind a shed. The feelings of guilt for stealing weighed on him but he saw no other way to walk around unnoticed. He didn't want to bring attention to himself and compromise his plan to find and hopefully rescue Marie.

The city looked like a different world than the Paris he knew. The streets were unrecognizable and not laid out in any sort of orderly fashion. Everything seemed to have been thrown together haphazardly. Some of the buildings looked vaguely familiar but were crowded so closely together that it was impossible for him to find his way.

The streets were a maze of twists and turns, so instead Ben searched for the river. The Seine was certainly the center; the entire city was built along its banks. If he could follow the river, he would get a sense of where he was and hopefully find his way to the Tuileries Palace.

As the sun rose, so did the people, and a sad, pathetic mass of humanity they were. They appeared tired, overworked and hungry. The women looked haggard. The children wore sadness on their gaunt faces. It was hard to believe that his Marie had lived her life in this time.

It was all Ben could do not to show repulsion at what he saw as he continued on. The living conditions in the city were deplorable. Rats ran freely along the alleys and pesky flies buzzed loudly around his body. He passed by food vendors working out of crude wooden carts. Although he was hungry, there was no way he would eat anything he saw, especially when he observed the filthy hands that served it up. He readjusted his medical bag, still slung across his shoulder, and was thankful to have it. He did his best not to be exposed to the people around him, but he had no choice. He knew disease was widespread, and there were few cures for many of the ills of this century.

The river came into view up ahead and for that, Ben was relieved. He imagined the morning sun sparkling on the water, but what he saw and smelled instead sickened him. The river was being used as a dumping ground for trash, sewage, and all sorts of vile things. Depression came over him in a wave. He had been so focused on Marie that he hadn't given much thought to his own fate. *What if I get stuck here, in the 1700's?* There were no promises he would ever get back. The thought almost sent him into despair, but he moved on, focusing on the task at hand.

Along the river he walked in the general direction of the Louvre, knowing that the Tuileries Palace once stood near there. The walkway was crowded, people constantly bumped into him. Many of the individuals he saw looked sick, with their bloodshot eyes and ashen skin. The children were the hardest to look at. There was an absence of the natural healthy glow children normally have, and their demeanor was downcast, not playful.

Finally, up ahead, Ben saw the Tuileries Gardens he knew so well. Only now, right in the middle, stood a massive ornate palace. He had no idea what he would find, and had made no plans as to what he would do when he got there.

Ben finally arrived and stood near the fence at one end of the palace. Immediately, he heard all he needed to hear. A small gathering of women began yelling through the fence, "Come out queen, we want to see you. Come out now! Stop hiding behind your royal robes. You're no better than us." Ben's heart soared just at the mention of her. She was here, somewhere just beyond the fence!

All at once there was a commotion. He heard a woman screaming and instinctively he turned towards her cries. Next to her, on the hard-packed dirt walkway, a man had collapsed. Ben immediately ran over, knelt beside the man, and assessed his physical condition. It was obvious he was in cardiac arrest and needed immediate CPR. The putrid smell of the man did not deter Ben from acting. He administered mouth to mouth and chest pumps. It took multiple tries, but finally the man recovered consciousness. The woman stared at Ben in shock.

She had never witnessed such a thing in all her life. When Ben rose from crouching over the man's body, he knew he was in trouble. A large crowd had gathered. He looked at the woman, nodded, and quietly told her to get the man to a doctor, then rushed into a small grove of trees and retched.

Kneeling in the grass he tried to recover, visibly shaken both emotionally and physically. Now he had exposed himself not only to the public eye, but also to untold germs and possible infection of any number of diseases. His throat burned. He needed water, clean water. *Where can I find clean water?* Ben knew the very basics of life he normally took for granted would be difficult to come by. As he slowly stood to his feet, he noticed two men standing off to the side, watching him. They were well dressed, not in the peasant garb that many others wore. Not wanting to engage them in conversation, Ben turned and walked towards the river. He felt their eyes on him as he walked. As he quickened his steps, they called out to him, "Monsieur, Monsieur!"

Ben turned. He knew it was useless to ignore them, and he thought stopping and talking to them for a moment would cause less of a stir than running away.

"Yes?"

"Who are you? Where do you come from?" asked the older of the two.

"I come from the country."

"Are you a doctor?"

"No."

The stranger paused, eyeing Ben carefully, "What was that back there, with that man? What were you doing?"

"I just helped him, that's all." Ben turned to walk away.

"Wait! I don't mean to pry. I'm a doctor. There are overwhelming needs here in the city. If you are a doctor, I could use your help."

"What do you mean?"

"There are very few of us here. We treat the sick when and where we can. The needs are staggering. We lack basic supplies and medicine. An extra set of hands would be most helpful."

Ben quickly assessed his situation. Perhaps this was his way to food and shelter. Once his basic needs were met, he would figure out a way to get to Marie. He chose his next words carefully, "I'm not a doctor, but I do have training. I would need a place to stay. I'm just passing through, but possibly I could stay and help for a while."

"Excellent. I'm Pierre Dubois and this is my assistant, Hugo Dupont. I have an apartment with an extra room above my office. You may stay with me for the time being."

"Thank you." Ben managed to respond, realizing he would have to be careful not to reveal the truth. Knowing the climate of the times, he imagined it wouldn't take much to be arrested, tried, imprisoned, or worse.

"Follow us."

They traveled on foot through the city to Rue Matignon, northwest of the Tuileries. Ben found the area much nicer than he expected, and was relieved when they stopped in front of a presentable apartment building. A wooden sign, with a mortar and pestle painted on it, swung back and forth in the breeze. They entered on the ground floor into a clinic. In the back was a spiral staircase that took one up to the living area. It was surprisingly clean. The furnishings were simple yet comfortable.

The two men invited Ben to sit down to a lunch of bread, dried meat, and wine. Dr. Dubois explained the difficulties of practicing medicine in Paris. The shortage of proper surgical instruments, medicines, and money were just some of the obstacles. Although this building was cleaner than what he saw outside, the smell remained. Despite that, Ben was grateful for a place to stay and food to eat. He would use this as home base until he could contact Marie, and hopefully somehow, they could return to the future.

Chapter 32

1791

Robespierre rode into Paris after only spending one day in the town of Versailles. He found he didn't need any further treatment for his leg, as it was healing miraculously, like nothing he had ever experienced before. While in a café, he found out he had been gone only two weeks. Nothing had changed while he was away. The guillotine continued in use, and for that he was happy. In his eyes, the only way to achieve lasting change was to remove anyone suspected of being against the new form of government they were trying to initiate.

Riding through the streets, he kept a constant watch for Ben. He was nowhere to be seen. As unsettling as that was, he was relieved to find his apartment near the Palais Royal exactly as he had left it. Nothing seemed amiss. No one had really noticed his absence, as he was known to visit his childhood home in Arras for weeks at a time. His apartment was simple, but adequate. He didn't believe in being surrounded by finery, even though his salary as a lawyer would have allowed him to live more comfortably.

He changed clothes, and headed to the café Le Procope, where every evening extensive political discussions were held. Times in

Paris were extremely difficult, and it was well known that Robespierre and his followers wanted big changes. Unfortunately for them, the changes were not coming fast enough. The royals were holding on to power any way that they could. The enormous strides the citizens made with the storming of the Bastille, and the subsequent arrest of the king and queen happened over two years ago. Robespierre was convinced the monarchy had to be eliminated sooner, rather than later.

Even he had to admit that Marie Antoinette had become his obsession. The very reason he had made the trek out to Versailles in the first place was his eerie fascination with her. He had wanted to go through her rooms in the palace and see if any piece of her remained... a token, a hairbrush, a shoe, anything. His obsession consumed him. In an odd way, he admired her strength, yet he found it threatening. *Yes, she along with Louis must die*, he thought, *it's the only way to safeguard the future of the new government of France*. He must find a way to convince the others. He wanted history to play out as he had read on the plaque in the square. He wished once again that he had been able to find out more about the past while he was in the future, but he was so focused on survival, he hadn't sought it out. *Never mind that*, he thought, *I have the here and now, and I will cause events to happen as I want them to*. He felt a great sense of power as he walked. *The monarchy must be punished for all the past sins they committed while in power*. He also wanted to secure his own position of power and influence. He licked his lips as he entered the café to start yet another debate about the future of the monarchy.

Chapter 33

1791

Standing at the window, Marie gazed out onto the courtyard of her prison. The Tuileries palace and gardens had long ago been abandoned by royalty and was now home to servants, their families, guards, prostitutes, and anyone else that dared take up residence in the run-down structure. It had been two years since the Royal family left Versailles under armed guards and had been escorted to Paris like common criminals. Figuratively, Louis and Marie were still king and queen, but they were being held against their will. The movement to remove them from power was underway.

As time dragged on, Louis tried repeatedly to speak to various groups, trying to secure a future for the monarchy. But it was useless. They refused to listen, or negotiate. As his political clout and supporters dwindled, so did his confidence. Paris was crawling with different factions, holding clandestine political meetings. No one knew who to trust, or who would end up in power when this reign of terror was over. The commoners were ready for a new form of government, no matter what form it took. Those hoping to end up in charge knew how to take advantage of the poor and their suffering.

As Louis became more and more despondent and depressed, Marie focused all her attention on the children. Her precious children—they kept her going. She did all she could to keep them occupied and happy. A tutor came in daily to give them their lessons and they took walks on the palace grounds for fresh air and exercise. Some days these walks were pleasant, some days they were cut short due to the prying eyes of the public. With the new political climate, commoners were allowed quite close to the monarchy. Only a wrought iron fence separated the palace area from the public. Sometimes citizens came out of curiosity, but other times they came just to hurl insults at the royal family, making them feel like caged animals. Armed guards followed them everywhere they went. Their conversations had to be held in hushed tones so as not to be overheard.

They were allowed visitors, but slowly their friends and family members became distant, afraid to be seen as royal sympathizers. Most of them had fled the country when they had the chance. Marie understood they were afraid for their safety, but the sting was there nonetheless. Her world now consisted of Louis, the children, a few close friends, and a handful of personal servants.

In time, Marie was forced to make all the political decisions behind the scenes for her and her family. She was completely ill equipped to be in this position, but in this position, she was. She slowly lost all respect for her husband. Louis had retreated into his own world, unable to cope. Frustration often showed on her face, but Louis did not seem to notice. She managed to keep quiet on the outside, and appear completely supportive. If it hadn't been for her children, she would have collapsed under the pressure, but she remained strong.

Depressed as she was at times, Marie still held out hope that the nightmare would end. She wrote letters imploring heads of state from other countries to come to their aid. Some tried, but their actions were futile against the Republic leaders. Louis and Marie had committed no crimes as king and queen, but that didn't matter. They continued to be held without charge.

Then the real terror began. In the beginning, the executions were few, but quickly increased in number. The dreaded guillotine was now in constant use. A person did not have to be proven guilty; just an accusation of being an enemy of the movement was enough for arrest and imprisonment. The trials were quick; the accused was allowed no council. Immediately following a trial, the prisoner was loaded onto a cart, taken to the guillotine and beheaded. The stench of death loomed heavy in the air, and blood literally ran between the cobblestones. Marie and Louis lived with this knowledge hanging over the heads daily.

However, there was one man working hard behind the scenes to free the Royal family, their long-time friend, Axel Ferson. Axel never lost his fondness for Marie and he returned to Paris after hearing of her imprisonment. He visited the couple at the Tuileries on occasion, but not enough to arouse suspicion. Soon Axel devised a plan for their escape. It would be extremely risky, but it was the only way to save their lives. He kept the plan to himself until he felt everything was ready. He did not want to give them false hope.

Chapter 34

Ben was thrust into caring for the sick almost immediately upon settling in at his temporary home. People far and wide knew of the elderly doctor, and word of his young, new partner spread quickly. Dr. Dubois often studied Ben, noting his unconventional ways, and the unusual speed and confidence with which he worked. He also noted Ben's peculiar insistence on cleanliness, constantly washing his hands. *Odd*, thought the doctor.

Each time Ben was paid for his work, he offered a few coins to Pierre, but carefully saved the rest. He ate little and often refused to drink the water, instead sticking to beer or wine. During his first few days, he had little opportunity to get out. He thought at first that this wasted time, but listening to conversations all around him, he continued to learn more and more about Marie and Louis. Just as the history books said, the common people blamed the royals for all the problems in the country: debt, hunger, drought, and mainly the lack of bread—which was actually due to poor crops. He did take careful note that Pierre never engaged in conversations about the royal family. He suspected that the good doctor was a royal sympathizer, but never admitted it openly.

Ben racked his brain to try and remember French history. He knew what events transpired in generalities, but not specific dates. Each night as he dropped into bed exhausted, he searched his memory for clues. He slowly pieced together the coming events and he knew he had little time. He must get to Marie as soon as possible.

By day four, Ben was ready to return to the Tuileries. He told Pierre he needed to run an errand. Although puzzled over Ben's strange ways and personality, he was so thankful for an extra pair of hands, that he didn't ask any questions.

Traveling on foot, Ben headed out. The streets were crowded, but he kept his head down, moving this way and that to avoid bumping into the others. He wasn't sure how he would do it, but seeing Marie was all that mattered to him. Once he could communicate with her, he was sure that somehow, things would work out. Not only did he wish to rescue her from prison and the dangerous city Paris had become, but to touch her, feel her, and be with her. He had so many questions. *If she just traveled back in time a few days ago, how is she in prison at the Tuileries? What has happened? How did she go from dauphine to queen? How did she explain her absence?* Just thinking about it made his head ache. He felt desperate to put his arms around her, to comfort her, certain she needed him as badly as he needed her.

Turning left and right through the maze of dirty, narrow streets, Ben soon realized he was lost. He had no idea which direction to turn to get to the Tuileries. At each corner he searched up and down the roads hoping for a glimpse of the river. He asked an elderly gentleman which way to the Seine, and the man nodded his head forward and Ben continued on.

Before long, he heard the faint sound of drumbeats. *What in the world is that,* he wondered. The sound was coming from up ahead, so he pressed on. The drums got louder and louder as he traveled, and suddenly, he came to a large square full of people. To his horror, up ahead, he saw it—a guillotine positioned atop a large wooden platform. The drummers were stationed to the left of the stand and to the right was a set of stairs that led up to the guillotine. He turned away, afraid of what he might see.

Moments later, the drums fell silent. Curious, he looked up, just in time to see the razor-sharp blade glimmer in the sunlight as it slid down its track. What Ben witnessed in that moment was horrific. His mind could not make sense of what his eyes had just seen—a person's head totally sliced from their body in a split second. He turned away again just as a loud cheer rang out from the crowd. The victim's head was being held up by the hair and paraded around the platform for all to see. His stomach turned, but he managed to keep going, anxious to escape the nightmare.

He arrived at the Tuileries and sat down on a bench by the fence to catch his breath and compose himself. Now his desire to get to Marie was stronger than ever. Not thinking too far ahead, he got up and walked straight up to the guards at the main entrance. "I would like to see the queen."

The guard looked at him incredulously, "What makes you think you can see the queen?"

"We are acquaintances."

"If you want to see the queen, you can see her like everyone else, through the fence when she takes her daily walk."

"When would that be?"

"What's it to you?"

"Please sir, when would that be?"

"Once in the morning, and again in the afternoon. Now step back. Be gone with you."

"Thank you, sir." Looking up, the sun was high in the sky, around noon he guessed. He would have to wait. He walked across the way into the surrounding park, found a shady spot underneath a tree and leaned his back against the thick trunk. He was feeling run down, tired. He closed his eyes for just a few moments, and promptly fell asleep.

He woke to the sound of distant drumbeats, angry with himself that he had fallen asleep. Visions of the earlier execution ran through his mind. He looked around to see how others were reacting, and to his shock, no one seemed to be alarmed, or take notice the sound of the drums. *Is it so common that no one seems to care?* He scrambled over to the fence. There was no sign of Marie. *I hope I didn't miss her.*

The drums continued. Ben was thankful he couldn't hear them from his room at Dr. Dubois'. He went across the street and bought a baguette from a vendor and returned to his spot under the tree. When he noticed people gathering near the fence to the gardens, he rose and stood with the others, peering through the iron bars.

The gardens were beautiful. The palace may have been run down, but the grounds were well kept. He admired the perfect symmetry of the greenery surrounding a line of statues, as well as a lovely fountain in the middle of the wide walkway that cut through the center of the garden. The area was quite large. Ben noted several different entrances to the garden and wondered if he might miss Marie all together, but there was nothing to do but stand and wait.

He was about to give up hope, when in the distance he saw three women walking together wearing fancy, ornate dresses, each carrying a parasol. They were walking towards him, but were still quite far away. He prayed one of them would be Marie. His heart pounded at the thought of seeing her again. Their circumstances were dreadful, and yet, he felt if they were reunited, there was a chance

Closer and closer the women came. From his vantage point, none of them looked anything like Marie. His heart sank. He couldn't believe it! He decided to go back to the guard and question him further. As he turned to go, he glanced once more at the trio. They were much closer to him now. The woman in the middle caught his attention, there was something very familiar about her walk. As he continued to watch her, he realized it was Marie.

No! It can't be! Gone were her youthful features. Her large blue eyes had lost their spark and her once lovely blonde hair was now a dull white. She had a sad, forlorn look in her eyes. He recognized that look, it was the same one she had when she spoke of her mother.

He continued to watch her as she walked towards him. *Why does she look so old? What has happened to her in the last few days?* Their eyes met. She paused briefly, and then walked on, as if he did not exist.

Chapter 35

Marie dined with Louis and the children that evening as was customary. They retired into the small living area, where Louis Charles and Marie Thérèse pulled out their favorite toy, a miniature wooden theater with hand-painted silk backdrops and tiny porcelain characters. Marie Thérèse often made up plays that they performed for their parents with remarkable skill. Tonight, was no exception. They performed a fairy tale, complete with an ogre, a dragon, and a prince that swooped in to save the princess. Marie couldn't help but smile at their creativity. Before leaving Versailles, Marie had had a tiny theater built near the Petite Trianon where she often put on plays for her friends. She was so proud to see her children show a love for theater.

Soon the children hugged and kissed their parents goodnight and were shuffled off to bed by their nurse. Louis lit the evening candles, and settled in to read. Marie sat down in a rocking chair with her needlework. Despite the enjoyable evening with the children, she felt an unusual sense of doom, and thought sewing might settle her mind. She felt a special need for it this particular evening. Her spirit was troubled; anxiety clung to her like dead weight.

She searched her mind trying to place the identity of the man she noticed peering through the fence during her afternoon walk. Thinking about him gave her an uncomfortable feeling, yet she couldn't get him out of her mind. He had looked at her so expectantly, like he knew her. The moment their eyes met, a feeling of déjà vu swept through her for just an instant. She tried to call it back, but it had evaporated completely. Thousands of people had visited Versailles over the years, so there was a strong possibility they had met before, but she couldn't place him. The expectant, then confused expression that crossed his face had puzzled her, and she wished she had not looked away so quickly.

Glancing down at her needlework, she realized she had not made a single stitch. Louis did not look up from his book when she slowly rose and walked over to the window. They were housed on the second floor of the palace, and often she stood at the small arched opening to catch a breeze or to look out across the gardens. She stared up at the moon, lost in thought, thinking of happier times when she had gazed at the moon from the balcony of her bedroom at her former home. Turning to go back to her needlework, a movement among the trees below caught her eye. She thought she saw someone looking up at her. She searched the garden intently, but decided it was her imagination. This was indeed an unsafe area at night. No one in his or her right mind would lurk around the gardens after dark.

Marie fell into a fitful sleep later that night, dreaming the same dream over and over. Like watching a play, she saw herself wearing a long white dressing gown, running through the woods in a dense fog. It seemed as if she was running away from something, as well as to something. Approaching the edge of the forest, she saw a man in the distance standing perfectly still. Not knowing who it was, and although frightened, she sensed he was there to help her. Nearing the shadowy figure and eager to see his face, he suddenly evaporated like a wisp of smoke. This dream repeated itself over and over. When the sun rose the next morning, she was grateful the night had ended.

All day long the dream haunted her. She went about her tasks and played with the children, but her mind was in the forest of her dreams. Later that afternoon during her walk, she found herself searching the fence for another glimpse of the man from yesterday. He never appeared.

That evening Axel Fersen came to visit. They were glad to see him, and exchanged pleasantries, but tonight he seemed unusually tense. Under the watchful eyes of the guards, he spoke in hushed tones. An escape plan was in the works to get them out of the country. As Axel went over the details, Louis bristled. The plan had them leaving the Tuileries under the cover of night disguised as an aristocratic family.

Louis immediately argued against the plan. He refused to be a king in exile, to run like a common criminal. He felt it imperative that they remain in Paris, or he feared they would lose the monarchy forever. Axel assured him that near the French border, a large army of royal sympathizers would be gathered for their protection. Louis could bargain from there with the leaders of the revolution, under the protection of the army.

After heartfelt persuasion from Marie, Louis finally relented. He insisted however, that they travel in the style they were accustomed, and arrive at the border in full royal regalia. He couldn't believe he was in such a position. It was not the French way. It seemed the memories of that terrifying night, when they were forcefully taken from Versailles, had faded from his mind. Even though they were imprisoned, he felt he would be able to regain his former glory.

"Perhaps it is possible to regain power from a safer distance, away from the savagery of Paris," Marie suggested. Her pleas were the only thing that swayed him.

Axel promised to return a few nights later with more details. For now, he kissed Marie goodbye on the hand, nodded to Louis, and left. His visit had not aroused any suspicion, being known as a long-time friend of the family, and a diplomat as well. Marie felt immense relief when she went to bed that night. This was the first glimpse of hope presented to them in over two years.

Chapter 36

The following morning, Robespierre woke up and jumped out of bed with a spring in his step. His time spent at café Le Procope the night before had been fruitful. He and the other leaders of the revolution gathered in one of the back rooms of the restaurant, staying well past midnight. The candles burned low as he made his case that the king and queen must be put to death.

They would not be persuaded so fast. The ancient regime had been in power for the past three hundred years, and even though the group desired a permanent change to the structure of their government, to kill the king and his wife seemed one step too far. Robespierre spoke with passion, and although the group did not come to an agreement, he had planted a seed that he felt sure would grow.

This goal became his driving force, the only thing that kept him sane. Every night he laid awake in the darkness, trying to understand how he had traveled to the future. He tried to convince himself it didn't really happen, but he knew better. It had been real. *But how? How did Marie come through the door and not be on the other side with Ben and me? How did she end up in the Tuileries?* These questions had gnawed at him over the past few days. He decided it was time... time to see her face to face.

Looking into the cloudy mirror over his chest of drawers, he pulled his white wig expertly over his bald head. He doused himself with flower water, and took extra care straightening his white dress shirt and waistcoat. Although small in stature, he wanted to look especially stately when he addressed the queen. He wanted to instill fear in her heart and mind, and remind her who was now in control.

Before going out the door, he picked up the letter he had written the night before to his long-time friend, Jean Baptiste Delambre, telling him about his passage through time. He folded it twice and laid it on the desk. He then placed a small ball of dark red wax into a spoon, and held it carefully over a burning candle. Once the wax melted, he poured it over the folded letter, and pressed his ring into the puddle of wax. The letter, now sealed, was tucked into the front pocket of his waistcoat. He then placed his three-cornered hat atop his head, and made his way to post the letter. He hoped his friend would get back to him soon, even though the contents of the letter would be shocking. His hope was that his friend would accept his invitation and make his way to Paris. He wanted to discuss his incredible experience, and share his description of the 21st century. He doubted he would be believed, but he had no one else he felt he could trust with such an outlandish story. Hopefully, his friend would come out of curiosity, if nothing else.

As he made his way to the Tuileries, he passed through his now favorite place in the city. Before the revolution, the square was known as Place of Louis XV, and in the center, was a magnificent statue of the former king on his horse. Once the revolution started, the statue had been pulled down, a wooden platform constructed in its place, and the square was renamed, Place de la Révolution. The guillotine had been placed on an elevated platform, so the beheadings could be seen from a great distance. It was positioned there to instill fear in the citizens of Paris. His chest puffed with pride as he walked through the square and thought of all those who died there, those he felt deserved death, because of their loyalty to the throne.

Soon he approached the Tuileries, licking his lips, a nervous habit he had acquired over the past few weeks. His cheeks and lips were a deep rose color, which contrasted against his pale white skin and wig, giving him a clown-like appearance.

He was almost giddy as he spoke to the guards to request an audience with the queen. It was an odd request for him to ask to see the queen instead of the king, but he was escorted promptly into a small reception area where the king and queen received visitors. For political meetings, Louis was usually summoned alone to another location, but today would be different. Today's meeting was of a personal nature between Robespierre and Marie.

Chapter 37

There was a sharp knock at the door to the apartments where the royal family was held. Louis looked over at Marie, and then nodded his head for the nurse to lead the children to another room. He answered the door promptly while Marie stayed seated on the couch where she had been reading. Standing erect at the door was one of the guards, "Excuse me sir, Maximilien de Robespierre requests an audience with the queen."

"There are no appointments scheduled for today," said Louis. When the guard stood in silence, Louis finally relented, "We will come in a moment."

"No, sir, he wishes to speak with her alone."

"Alone?" said Louis. He turned to Marie and she shrugged her shoulders.

"I will go," she said.

"Are you sure, Marie? You know what he stands for."

"I know, Louis. I am not afraid. We have committed no crimes. I will hear what he has to say."

Marie had seen Robespierre only once at a reception held at Versailles about six months before her arrest. She remembered him as shy, standing off on his own, not engaging anyone around him. What struck her then were his eyes. They were extremely small, and along with his pointy nose, his features resembled that of a mouse. She knew he was now one of the leaders of the revolution, but she hadn't seen him face to face since coming to the Tuileries. Louis, of course, had met with him and the other members of the movement numerous times, as they pretended to listen to his opinions about the future of France. She nervously descended the stairs to the bottom floor of their section of the palace and into the room where Robespierre waited.

Since they had never been formally introduced, she held her hand out to him as she approached. He stared into her eyes with a shocked expression on his face. He opened his mouth to speak, and stopped. He seemed confused. He waited for her to speak.

"Bonjour, Monsieur Robespierre," said Marie. "What is the nature of your visit?"

He continued to gawk at her, baffled, not understanding how she had aged so much since he saw her just a few days ago. He was also shocked at her behavior. How was it that she pretended not to know him, to remember their encounters?

"Nice to see you, Madame Antoinette. But surely you remember me from a few days ago."

"I have no idea what you're talking about."

"Of course, you do. My question is, how did you get back here to the Tuileries from Versailles? How did you age? What has happened?"

Marie felt a flash of memory slice through her body. She turned away from him, feeling desperate to get out of the room. She didn't remember any details, but suddenly she knew they had met, and she immediately felt threatened. She felt he knew things about her that even she herself could not recall.

"Madame, has he come to you?"

Another flash of memory went through Marie like a shot, but was gone before she could grab onto it. Marie swallowed hard. She slowly turned back to him, but kept her eyes to the floor. "Has who come to me? I have no idea what you're talking about. I must go." With that, she turned and headed for the door. Just before she crossed the threshold, he grabbed her wrist and jerked her around to look at him. Fear gripped her so tightly she couldn't breathe. There was something so familiar about this moment; she felt she had been in this exact position before. "Unhand me immediately! Guards! Guards!"

Instantly 3 guards filled the room, and Robespierre had no choice but to let go. Marie fled. He stood frozen to his spot. The meeting had not gone as planned. He had gone in with such high expectations, so sure he would intimidate her, sure she would speak to him about their shared experience. Now he felt vulnerable and insecure. *Did it really happen? Am I going mad? She did not seem to know me, to remember anything.*

Slowly he regained his composure and began his journey home. As he walked back through the square, the drums began to beat, and a cart containing the next guillotine victim rolled right in front of him, almost running over his foot. He jumped back just in time and looked up into the eyes of a beautiful young woman, an aristocrat with long brown hair, tears staining her porcelain cheeks. He looked away quickly, feeling for the first time ill-equipped to cope with the new realities he had helped create in the country he loved.

Once back at his apartment he paced back and forth, talking out loud, assuring himself he was okay, he was not crazy, that the events he remembered really did happen. Marie had to be lying, not wanting to admit their previous encounters. He knew of her impending death, he had read about it with his own eyes on the plaque in the very square he had just passed through on his way home. She was frightened, he was sure of it. That had to be the reason she acted dumbfounded by his questions. *She's afraid. She knows her fate. She is trying to confuse me.* He decided he had to locate Ben as soon as possible, but how?

Chapter 38

Ben stood under a tree near the Tuileries, trying to make sense of what just happened. He gently reached into his pocket and felt for the rosary, the only concrete item that still linked him to Marie. Absentmindedly he rubbed the cross between his fingers. The woman walking in the garden had been Marie, he was sure of it. *How did she age? Why did she not recognize me?* He stayed until sundown, hoping to get another glimpse of her.

As night fell, he walked around the fence to the opposite side of the garden. He noticed a light up above and was shocked to see Marie standing at the window, gazing up at the stars. He thought for a moment she saw him in the moonlight, but she quickly turned away. He decided to go back to his room. He had done all he could do for today.

Walking home through the dark streets should have scared him, but his thoughts were not on the here and now, they were on his situation. As the full implications weighed on him, his legs began to shake, causing his gait to weave back and forth. *What am I doing here? If Marie doesn't know me, why should I stay?* Just as quickly another thought hit him. *How will I ever get back? Should I return to Versailles and go back through the door? Would that even work? Is the door the answer, the pathway back to the future?*

What about Marie's appearance? When she stepped back in time, did she age instantly? Why doesn't she remember me?

He quickly calculated in his head. *She was born in 1755, which means she is now 35. Has she lived out her life as if we never met?* The questions had no answers. He was mentally and physically exhausted. As he rounded the corner to the apartment building, he felt lightheaded. He hadn't eaten much all day and he felt weak, dizzy. He barely spoke to the doctor when he walked in, instead going straight up the stairs to his room where he dropped into his bed and passed out.

Hours later, Ben woke up in a pool of sweat. His skin was on fire, fever ravaging his body. What he had feared most had happened. He was sick, horribly sick, and he knew he was in extreme danger. *People die easily here, disease is widespread, and now I'm sick. I could die.* He tossed and turned all night with fever. His lips became swollen and puffy. He was too weak to move, even too weak to dampen his mouth with water.

When Ben failed to come down the next morning, Dr. Dubois knocked on his bedroom door. When there was no answer, he opened the door and immediately saw how ill Ben was.

"My God Ben, what's wrong? What is it?"

"I don't know exactly. I'm... so hot."

"I'll get my instruments and examine you."

"No, I'll be all right if I stay in bed and rest. Could you reach in my bag please, and hand me the green bottle?" Ben knew he wasn't interested in any of the remedies Dr. Dubois had available, but a few aspirin might help. "Could you also hand me the clear bottle as well?" Ben took 2 aspirins and an antibiotic. At this point, he wished he hadn't wasted the stronger antibiotic on Robespierre. *This will have to do,* he thought. Pierre placed a cool cloth on Ben's forehead, and when the doctor offered him water, he drank it down greedily.

However, he did not recover. In fact, he got worse. For two days and nights fever continued. Pierre became increasingly concerned, but Ben refused any treatment. The doctor tried in vain to apply leeches to Ben's body, a known remedy at the time, but Ben would have none of it. All the doctor could do was come upstairs a few times a day to spoon feed Ben some soup, and try to make him as comfortable as possible.

On the third night, delirious with fever, Ben's head throbbed. He couldn't get any fresh air to cool himself as the windows were shut tight. What he would have given to stick his head outside for a deep breath, but he was just too weak.

There was a knock at the door downstairs. Pierre answered, welcoming a man in with open arms, inviting him upstairs. Ben's door being slightly ajar, allowed him to see the men sit down at a small wooden table, and he watched as Pierre poured them each a glass of port. After a few pleasantries, the conversation turned serious. Ben could barely make out their words. To his shock, he heard Pierre call the other man Axel. *Could it be? Could this possibly be Axel Ferson?* Ben listened carefully, but only heard bits and pieces of the conversation.

"When will you carry out the plan?" asked Pierre.

"Very soon, perhaps as early as Sunday night. I'm awaiting word that all is ready. The horses along the route have been secured. One difficulty is the king's insistence on traveling with his robes and crown, jewelry, books, and other personal items. He is blind to the gravity of their situation. He doesn't realize we are trying to save his life, and the lives of his family. He thinks we are focused on saving the regime, to return him to power. First, we must get them to safety, and if the monarchy is to be restored, it will happen in time."

"How will you handle all the provisions the king is insisting on bringing?"

"Part of it will be left behind. By the time he realizes, it will be too late. He will have no choice but to continue without them. We have had a carriage built with special compartments under the seats to hide some of the items that would give them away as the royal family. The queen's governess will take on the role of a Russian baroness. Marie and Louis' sister will travel as her maids. Louis will act as her butler. Louis Charles will wear a wig, so both children will be traveling as the baroness's daughters."

"Sounds like you've thought of everything. I just wish the carriage was smaller, less noticeable."

"Of course, but this is the best we could do. I've come by to thank you for your generous support, and for your friendship. The king will be told of your contributions of course."

"Thank you. I'm glad to be of service. If you think of anything else, let me know. I am at your disposal."

Ben could not believe his ears. *This must be the escape attempt I read about back at the apartment!* It seemed history was definitely repeating itself. *Monday is only two days away!* He knew the tragic outcome, that they would not make it, and ultimately, this escape attempt would seal their fate. *I have to warn them. I must tell them what I know!*

Just as Axel stood to leave, Ben called out, but in his weakened condition, his voice was but a whisper. He panicked. He had to get to Axel before it was too late. He swung his legs over the side of the bed, and stood up slowly. He took one step, and collapsed. Pierre heard the fall as he closed the door behind Axel, and he rushed back upstairs to find Ben on the floor. He awkwardly pulled him back onto the bed, covered him with a blanket and left him to sleep for the rest of the night.

Chapter 39

Marie had been a wreck for days now and Louis was worried about her. She seemed agitated, fearful, ever since her visit with Robespierre. When he asked her what happened, she refused to speak of it, becoming increasingly upset whenever he brought it up. Finally, he stopped asking. He thought back to that horrible time all those years ago when he thought she was losing her mind. Her behavior now reminded him of that time, and it frightened him. She had been a pillar of strength throughout their imprisonment. Without her to lean on, he felt he would not be able to cope.

Marie could barely eat or sleep. She constantly tried to pull her veiled memories up to the surface, but they refused to come. She knew a part of her life was missing from her memory. She had had the same feeling many times over the years, and now, since the visit with Robespierre, she was sure of it.

Axel came to the Tuileries on Sunday evening to inform Louis all was ready for the escape. He had word that the troops were assembled, prepared to receive the king and queen. They would leave at midnight.

Axel left quickly. He had a few more details to attend to. This operation had taken months of preparation and planning, along with large financial contributions from anonymous sources. They had been careful whom they had asked to help along the journey. Many citizens wore red and blue ribbons on their clothing as a show of support for the revolution, whether they believed in the cause or not. It was a way to blend in, to be accepted. It was difficult to know whom to trust. Anyone connected in any way to the royal family was suspect, most preferring to stay undercover. Almost all the courtiers, noblemen, dukes and duchesses had left the country, and finally the royal couple was ready to leave France as well.

Louis and Marie spoke that evening in hushed tones under candlelight. They decided not to tell the children about the plan until they woke them up to leave. They would then impress upon them not to speak or say anything to anyone along the journey. Something as simple as their way of speaking, could give them away. Marie tucked the children in, and kissed them goodnight. She lingered at their bedside, studying their innocent little faces, knowing that tonight their lives would change yet again. She returned to the other room, and Louis suggested she lie down. "We have a long night ahead of us; it's hours before our departure."

Marie went to bed staring at the candle wax as it slowly dripped down the taper. She felt she would suffocate from fear, and yet despite her anxiousness, she dropped off to sleep. The dream began again, only this time, when she approached the man in the clearing, he did not disappear. Suddenly, she recognized him! It was the same man she had seen staring at her in the garden days before. He looked deep into her eyes. Her mind swam in confusion at first, then suddenly, she knew! "Ben!" she cried.

"Yes, it's me. I've come for you."

"Oh, Ben, I've missed you so." They embraced, and all the fears in her heart melted away.

"I've missed you too, but we must hurry."

"Why? What's wrong?"

As Ben opened his mouth to speak, Marie woke up. Startled by the dream, she got out of bed and paced around the room, walking in circles. This time the dream was so vivid, so real. Who was this Ben, and why had he come to her in the dream? Why was she drawn to him? And most important, why was he familiar enough to her, that she called him by name? She had never seen the man in the garden before, so why had he made such an impact on her that he entered her dreams? She pondered these thoughts as she paced, afraid to go back to sleep. Finally, she prepared to leave, making last minute checks to the small bags they had packed for the trip.

As she examined the few things she would be able to take with her, her eyes misted over. She thought back to when she crossed the border into France as a young teenage girl. She remembered the desperate feeling she had had, as one by one her possessions were taken, and how her precious dog had been wrenched from her clutches as she cried silent tears.

Similarly, the night they were forced from Versailles, there was not time to pick and choose what she would bring with her. Her maids had made all the decisions in a rush, throwing their things into trunks without much thought. Heartbroken, she remembered how devastated Marie Thérèse had been when they realized her favorite doll had been left behind in the chaos.

Now, once again, she was being forced to leave most of her memories behind. The more Marie thought about it, the angrier she became. Feelings she had stuffed down for years bubbled to the surface. *I won't do it this time, I won't!*

She grabbed the candlestick from her nightstand and made her way to a room they used for storage. It was located down the hall at the top of a small set of stairs. Most of their trunks had been stored there. They had quickly gone through some of their belongings when they first arrived at the Tuileries, but it had been so overwhelming and painful at the time, that they had only unpacked the bare necessities. They had little need of the royal accouterments and keepsakes, eventually storing them away, out of sight.

She opened the door to the room, and raised her candle high in the air. She was shocked at how many trunks and boxes still remained. She would have to work quickly. She pulled only a few of her monogrammed trunks out into the open area by the door. Unfastening the golden latch of the first trunk was like going back in time. Tears streamed down her face as she looked at some of her old dresses, shoes, hats, and jewelry. She knew once she and Louis made their escape, anything left behind would be pawed through, stolen, and sold to the highest bidder. It had happened at Versailles, and it most certainly would happen here the same way.

A feeling in her spirit rose up, and she took charge. She quickly chose small items that could be carried easily. Ultimately, she decided the only things she could safely bring with her were some pieces from her personal jewelry collection. She chose around 10 items, wanting to preserve some for herself and some for her daughter. Digging through the second trunk, she came across a small chest. She opened it, and found it full of solid gold coins, engraved with her husband's likeness. She decided to save a few of these for Louis Charles. She wanted him to always remember his father as king, no matter what happened to them in the future.

It wasn't that she wanted to hoard the items for their monetary value. She wanted to preserve the memories, to feel like she had some control over her life. As she pulled one last trunk out to inspect it, she noticed a blue silk box slightly crumpled in the corner. Something about the box drew her to it, and the now familiar feeling of déjà vu came over her. As she reached for the box, Louis came through the door. "Marie, what are you doing? It's time to wake the children and dress them for the journey. What are you looking for?"

"I just wanted to gather a few personal remembrances Louis, a few keepsakes for the children."

"Please don't worry yourself about that. Once I'm restored to power, all these things will be returned to us. I've already given many of our things to Axel and his men, and they've been hidden in the coach. Come Marie, it's almost time."

"I'm bringing these things with me Louis. I must."

"But how? We have nowhere to hide them safely."

Marie thought quickly. "I will hide them somehow. No one will know."

"Well, do so quickly. We leave in half an hour."

The blue silk box forgotten, they returned to their bedroom and Marie immediately went to work, concealing the treasures into the folds of her petticoats.

Chapter 40

Ben opened his eyes slowly. Sunlight filled the room. Having no idea how long he had been asleep, he tried to remember the past few days. He knew he had been sick with a high fever, but it had now passed. Maybe he was through the worst of it. His tongue felt thick. He noticed a small bowl of water placed next to his bed, and vaguely remembered Pierre coming in and out of the room, periodically cooling his forehead with a wet cloth and insisting he take sips of water. He shuddered when he thought of the unclean liquid going into his body. Despite these unsettling thoughts, Ben's thirst overcame him, and he downed the remaining water in one gulp.

Through the open door of his room, he saw and heard no one. He got up, wobbling as he took his first few steps into the dining area and devoured some bread that was left on a plate. Out of energy, he leaned heavily against the wooden table as he managed to swallow the dry, crusty bread. He got a dipper of water out of the bucket on the counter, and drank it down fast. Again, wondering exactly how long he had been asleep.

He sat down in a chair at the table, and looking at the empty chair across from him, he suddenly remembered the visit from Axel. He jumped up, memories of the conversation flooding his mind. Realizing the escape attempt may have already happened, he hurried into his room to dress. Dizziness overcame him. He was forced to sit down to regain his equilibrium. He must find out what day it is. Even if Marie didn't know him any longer, he was desperate to save her. He couldn't bear the thought of her going to the guillotine. He knew this was his best chance to get to her, probably his only chance.

He decided to go to the Tuileries, to see if there was any word of their escape. He carefully made his way downstairs, and as he reached for the door handle, it turned. It was Dr. Dubois. When he saw Ben standing there, he was overjoyed.

"You're awake! I'm so happy to see you up."

Ben leaned into the door to steady himself. "Please... I must know... what day is it?"

"Why, it's Monday."

"Oh my God..." Ben stepped back, wondering where to begin. "It's hard to explain, but you must trust me. I have reason to believe the royal family is in danger."

Pierre looked at Ben pensively. He felt he could trust him, but what did he know, and how could he know it? Pierre kept his cool. "Whatever do you mean? The royal family is being held in the Tuileries."

"Listen Pierre, I'm on your side. I believe as you do that the king and queen should be freed, possibly even reinstated to the throne. But now is not the time to discuss that, they are in serious danger as we speak."

"What do you mean? What makes you think so?"

"I know the plan, the escape." Ben wanted to spill all his knowledge to his friend, but he was careful not to go too deeply into the story, knowing that would be disastrous. He had no time for a long explanation, especially one he didn't understand himself. "Please you must trust me. When do they plan to leave?" Even though Ben knew generalities, he did not remember any specifics of the escape, other than the name of the town, Varennes, where they would eventually be caught. Once that happened, Ben would have no way to help them.

"Ben, you must listen to me. Times are dangerous in Paris right now. You can't trust anyone. Whatever you think you know, you have to be sure of your source."

"I know about Axel. I know he has the carriage ready for them. I know the general route they are going to take. Please tell me, when are they leaving?"

Pierre raked his fingers through his hair. Finally, he said, "They've already left. Hours ago."

As the words came out, Ben grabbed the doctor's shirt. "Please, I must have a horse, a fast one. I must try to save them!"

"But Ben, that is unwise. If you go after them, you will expose them to grave danger. They will be found out."

"Don't you understand? They are already in grave danger. I'm their only hope."

The doctor sat down at the table to think. He had to sort all this out, but Ben would have none of it. "There is no time to lose. Please, we must act now."

With eyes closed Pierre finally spoke. "Very well. I know where you can get a horse. I'll take you there now."

Ben and Pierre left the apartment, and walked a few blocks heading south. Within minutes, they were standing in front of a livery stable. Ben stayed back, while the doctor spoke to the owner. They knew each other, so a horse was saddled up quickly.

The two men walked back to the apartment, and Pierre loaded a canvas bag up with bread, hard cheese, and some money. He also drew a crude map showing the route the family was planning to take. "They are traveling in a simple ride-for-hire coach until they reach Porte Saint-Martin. Once there, they will move to a much larger coach that Axel has waiting for them. They will use that coach for the rest of the journey." He shoved the paper and pencil into the bag and handed it to Ben. Before their final parting, the doctor embraced him and with tears in his eyes said simply, "Godspeed, my friend."

Fueled by adrenaline, Ben mounted the horse and was off. An ominous feeling filled the air as Pierre went back to his apartment. There was a chance he had just helped the royal family immensely, or had made the biggest mistake of his life.

Chapter 41

For days Robespierre had scoured the streets of Paris, looking for any sign of Ben. He inquired at cafés and bars, describing Ben as well as he could, but no one seemed to know anything. Finally, his luck changed early one morning when he entered a pharmacy to buy some salve. His scalp had developed a nasty rash due to the constant irritation from the wig he wore daily. The proprietor was in deep conversation with another customer. Robespierre waited impatiently, pacing about the room. Suddenly, the conversation took an interesting turn.

"Yes, he was in here the other day with Dr. Dubois. He was asking if we carried some substances I've never heard of. His accent was quite strange, and his appearance was, well, different."

"What do you mean?" asked the customer.

"I can't explain it. His mannerisms, the cadence of his speech, the look of his hair, it all seemed peculiar to me. A friend had recently told me of an extraordinary event he witnessed near the Tuileries. He told me a strange man saved the life of another by the most unusual method. Sure enough, just days ago, the doctor and the stranger walked in together. As soon as I saw them, I knew it had to be him."

"Strange indeed. Well, I've got to get back to my wife and give her this remedy."

"Let me know if she improves. Remember, three times a day."

"Yes, I won't forget. Good day."

"Good day."

Robespierre was stunned. He was sure the man was speaking of Ben. He immediately asked the proprietor the location of Dr. Dubois' office, and was happy to find out it was just a few blocks away. *Finally, a chance to find him!*

He hastily left the shop and was heading down the street when he heard conversation all around. Something had happened in Paris. Finally, he asked another man, "What has happened?"

"The king and his family have escaped. They are missing from the Tuileries."

"What do you mean?"

"This morning when the servants brought in their breakfast, they were gone. The guards have scoured the entire palace. They are nowhere to be found."

"Gone?"

"Yes. Disappeared into thin air. The guards are now searching the surrounding area."

"It can't be!" Robespierre was enraged. He hastened his steps to the doctor's building. He must find out if Ben was there. He knew Ben would somehow be connected to the disappearance. He must get the information as quickly as possible. *This will not happen. She will not escape. They both must die, even if I have to go after them myself,* he thought. It would jeopardize everything he had worked so hard for... the new government, his personal power and position, everything. No, he would not let this happen.

He walked straight into Dr. Dubois office without knocking. The doctor was busy with a patient, but glancing up, he recognized Robespierre immediately. A chill went through his body. He had seen and heard him making political speeches in the public arena many times over the past few years. The man was feared throughout Paris. Pierre's mind raced, wondering if the escape had been discovered. They had been gone less than twelve hours. *There is no way anyone can connect me to the escape. I've been extremely cautious... but someone must know something. Perhaps Ben shouldn't have been trusted. Maybe he's not the man I thought he was.*

"Where is your partner?"

The question surprised the doctor. How was Robespierre connected to Ben? "Who do you mean sir?"

"Ben."

"I've never heard of a Ben."

"Look, I know he's been working with you. Either tell me now, or you'll be under arrest before the sun sets."

"I'm sorry, I have no idea who you're talking about."

Robespierre scanned the room looking for any evidence he could find to tie the two together. He saw nothing out of the ordinary. He glanced over to the staircase and asked, "What's up there?"

"My living quarters."

"If you have nothing to hide, you won't mind me looking around up there will you?"

"You have no right."

"I have every right." With that he raced up the stairs with Dr. Dubois following close behind. The doctor closed his eyes and prayed as Robespierre went into Ben's room. He hoped nothing in there would give him away. He shuddered with a fear he had never felt in his life when out came the dreaded man with Ben's bag.

"I know this bag. I've seen Ben with it. Tell me now what you know," he shouted. "Where is he? What do you know about the disappearance of the king and queen?"

"I know nothing."

"You're lying. You will be imprisoned for treason. You will die if you do not tell me what you know." Dr. Dubois remained silent. Then and there he decided not to say another word, afraid he would further incriminate himself. *But how does Robespierre know there is a link between Ben and the royal family?* Not even he himself knew what the link was, and how Ben knew the things he did.

Exasperated at the doctor's silence, Robespierre sneered at him, and walked towards the door taking Ben's bag with him. Just before he left, he looked back and said, "You are a traitor to the revolutionary cause, and you know what happens to traitors. It will only be a matter of time." With that, he licked his lips and was off.

Immediately Robespierre rushed to the Tuileries to see for himself what exactly had transpired. He found the scene exactly as he had been told. Guards were scattered about with confused looks on their faces. He had to take control. He went into the offices of the Estates General and found most of the leaders present discussing the shocking turn of events. No one saw it coming. No one thought the weak king had it in him to try such a brazen act. Now they would have to act fast.

Robespierre immediately took control and called a meeting. He spoke with passion, putting himself in full charge of capturing and bringing back the king and queen. He called for a runner to go to his dwelling and have his horses and carriage made ready for travel. He assembled a band of soldiers to spread out along the roads leading out of Paris. All communication was to be brought back to him, and he mapped out the route he chose to take, and passed the information on to the ranking officers of each unit.

His carriage soon arrived, and all was made ready for the chase. Just before he closed the carriage door, he climbed back out and walked over to the group of soldiers that had been in charge of guarding the king and queen. "It's obvious you all are loyal to the king, or you would not have let this happen. There's only one way to save your heads. Go and find Dr. Dubois immediately. Take him to the Tower prison. See that he is beheaded before the sun goes down. I will return and see if you've carried out my wishes. For your sake, I hope you have." With that Robespierre got back in the carriage, and he and his guards were off on the chase of their lives.

Chapter 42

The coach lumbered down the road slowly. Wishing they could move faster, Marie stared out the window into the darkness, thinking back over the events of the past few days, and periodically glancing down at her children sleeping peacefully on the floor of the carriage. How easily children trusted their parents, even when sensing danger. She still felt guilt over not sending the children off to safety when they knew Versailles was going to be overrun. They had foolishly missed that opportunity. Her children had suffered for their decision, and she vowed this time it would be different. When Axel originally presented the plan to her, she knew it was a risk they had to take.

Convincing Louis had been difficult, but she knew the way to his heart. She had used his sense of duty to France, his God-given duty to uphold the monarchy, to persuade him to try and escape. Once he was convinced the escape wasn't to go into exile, but a way to regain power, he decided to risk it. At this very moment, troops were amassed near the border of France and Germany to welcome the king. From there, a plan could be devised to take France back from the revolutionaries and return their country and its people to some sense of normalcy. The violence in Paris had to stop, and Louis felt he was the only one to reestablish peace.

The previous day they had spoken in hushed tones, and the anxiety was such that even Marie Thérèse had felt it, and asked her mother repeatedly what was happening. She was assured all was well, and tucked into bed. Finally, at midnight, Marie and Louis gathered the children, dressed them in new clothes, and told them they were going on a great adventure, but that they must be very obedient and not speak to anyone, period. Louis Charles did not want to wear the itchy wig, but they convinced him it was like playing a part in a play, just like the ones his sister made up. He finally relented.

The others put on their disguises and slipped out a back entrance of the palace, and boarded the simple coach under the cover of darkness. Axel acted as coachman, driving them out of Paris. They were on their way to Porte Saint-Martin where the larger, more comfortable coach awaited them to take them on the rest of their journey. Marie continued staring out the window wondering, *Will we ever get there?*

Another hour went by before they halted to a stop. Axel jumped down and opened the carriage door. "We're here. Unload quickly and quietly into the other carriage."

Louis carried Marie Thérèse, and Marie lifted Louis Charles into her arms, and walked the short distance off the road to where the other carriage stood. The rest of the party followed. Once they were loaded up, Axel took the helm of this coach as well. Marie knew he wasn't traveling with them all the way to the border. How she wished he could stay with them for the entire journey. His confidence and intelligence made her feel safe and secure and it was only because of him and his leadership, that she was willing to put her family in such peril.

Into the night they traveled. The new coach was much roomier and more comfortable than the first one. Louis Charles again fell asleep on the floor at their feet, under her massive petticoats. Louis leaned against the window of the carriage and dozed off as well. Marie began to tire as she relaxed a bit. The weighty carriage moved slowly, and she knew it would be dark for many hours to come. Gradually she drifted off to sleep as well.

Within moments, a dream had her right back in the foggy meadow with Ben. Again, she approached him. Their conversation was the same at first and then... things changed.

"Marie, I've come for you. We must hurry."

"Why?"

"Because you are in grave danger. Don't you remember? You won't make it through the escape. You will be found out."

"No. It's all planned. We will be fine. What I don't understand is how you got here. Where have you been?"

As Ben was about to speak, the coach hit a rut in the road and jolted violently, and she opened her eyes. She shifted in her seat and drifted back to sleep, seeing herself in her mind's eye as strange events played out. She saw herself waking up in Versailles in the future, traveling to Paris, and all the wonderful times she had with Ben. She saw herself sitting in Ben's apartment reading a book, and suddenly became agitated. *What was the book? What was it about?* She thought and thought trying to remember. *Why is the thought of a book so upsetting?* Suddenly, she woke up again, wondering where have these scenes in her mind come from. She felt so confused; the stress and anxiety were finally taking a toll, even in her dreams.

As morning dawned, they pulled the carriage as far off the road as possible between towns. They stopped to rest the horses, stretch their legs, and have a quick meal. The children played chase as the adults nervously paced, watching up and down the road. The trip was going as planned. It was just ahead where Axel would leave them. He promised they would be in capable hands. Marie would be sad to see him go, but felt sure they would see him again.

She finally sat down and absentmindedly ate some bread, while her thoughts turned back to the night before. She felt like she would go mad if these dreams did not stop. She thought of Ben, this imaginary friend she was conjuring up in her mind and in her dreams. She did not know him, and was disturbed that he looked exactly like the man she had seen peering in from outside the garden fence. She had only seen him that one time, and still, his face continued to haunt her. She would be glad when they got to safety, and her nerves settled. She was sure once they were all safe and she was able to relax, the dreams would stop.

Chapter 43

Ben rode as fast as he could down the road toward the carriage. He couldn't travel at a full gallop in the dark, but he pushed the horse harder than he normally would have. He had to get to the next town, the spot where a new driver would take Axel's place. Ben thought if he could arrive before the coach, he could somehow intervene. He didn't know what he would say, or how he would announce himself, especially considering that Marie didn't remember him. He wasn't sure if she even remembered coming to the future. This confused him a great deal, because he had traveled through time as well, but remembered everything. He couldn't wait to get Marie alone, where he could talk to her, explain, and awaken her memory.

Of course, even if he reached her, there were problems. As much as he wanted to grab Marie, save her from being recaptured, and see if they could get back to the future, she now had her children with her. He couldn't ask her to leave them behind. There was Louis as well... would she be willing to leave him? Was it possible that Ben would be able to warn them, but in the end, still lose Marie completely?

He also knew any intervention could change the course of history. How will things play out, if Marie and Louis lived?

France would be changed forever, which would undoubtedly change his own future, and possibly his past. Ben's horse slowed, and his attention turned away from his thoughts and back to the task at hand. He had to find Marie first. He loved her, and that was enough. He would take his chances with the rest of the unknown.

His horse was exhausted, and as much as he wanted to keep pressing forward, he knew he had to stop and allow the horse some rest. He dismounted, stood in the stillness of the night, and distinctly heard water rushing nearby. He followed the sound, and under the light of the full moon, made his way to the stream. Both horse and rider bent down to drink. After satisfying their thirst, Ben tied the horse to a tree, where it found some green grass to eat. Ben sat down and leaned against the tree trunk, and before he knew it fell fast asleep, worn out from the journey and still not fully recovered from his illness. Had he been alert, he would have heard the large carriage pass by just beyond the trees where he slept.

Hours later, Ben squinted his eyes against the morning sun, and quickly jumped up. He had not planned to sleep at all, but certainly not until sunrise. He felt sick in his heart. His exhaustion may have greatly jeopardized his only hope of success.

His horse was still standing where he left him a few hours before. He untied him and off they went, galloping at a fast pace. It wasn't long until they reached the destination. *Has the carriage passed through here yet? How will I find out?* He slowly trotted his horse through the sleepy town in search of the carriage. He was about to give up hope, when he saw a familiar face coming towards him on another horse. Where had he seen that man before? As they passed on the road, the man nodded and tipped his hat. A moment later, he realized who it was. It was the man he had seen at Dr. Dubois' apartment the night of the fever. It was Axel Fersen! Ben knew he was close!

He turned his horse around, and caught up to Axel. "I was wondering, sir, do you know of a place where I could get some oats for my horse? I've been traveling all night, and he needs some nourishment."

"Yes. Continue on this road, and down to the left is a livery stable. They will have the supplies you need. Follow me, I'll show you."

Axel led Ben to the stable. The owner came out, surprised to see him again. "Is there anything else I can do for you Mr. Fersen? We thought you were well on your way."

"Yes, I was headed back to Paris, and met this young man on the road. He needs some oats for his horse."

"That I've got. Have a good trip back sir. You've done a good deed, you have."

"Thank you. I'll be seeing you." With that he tipped his hat to Ben, turned his horse around and trotted off down the road.

Ben knew then that the exchange had been made. Axel had finished his leg of the journey, and the carriage was even further down the road. Ben quickly paid for the oats and was off. He must hurry. He must intersect with them before they were discovered.

Ben rode on for perhaps an hour, pushing his horse as hard as he felt possible. He rounded a bend in the road and there before him, up ahead, was a huge coach moving along slowly. Ben carefully passed by, his heart pounding with anticipation.

Careful not to make eye contact, he stared straight ahead, acting as if they didn't interest him in the least. He rode on until he was out of sight, pulled his horse to a stop, and hid in a grove of trees. As he waited, he opened his bag and took a bite of bread. When he went to return the half-eaten loaf, he noticed the map the doctor had drawn for him, along with the pencil. That gave him an idea. If he could somehow get a note to Marie, perhaps he could jog her memory. He decided to wait for the carriage to pass, and follow at a safe distance until an opportunity presented itself. It was a risky plan, but short of going right up to them and saying, "I'm from the future," it was the only thing he could think of.

A few minutes later Ben heard the noise of the coach approaching. He watched as it slowly made its way past him, and then suddenly, it pulled off the road. He couldn't believe it! He watched as the coachmen climbed down. There seemed to be a problem with one of the wheels, and a long discussion ensued. Ben could hear only bits and pieces of the conversation. They were arguing whether to take time to change the wheel now, or take their chances and press on. Louis insisted they change it, that it would be too risky if they broke down in the middle of a town, or on a busier part of the road. Marie and children disembarked the coach, and walked around stretching their legs while the repair was made. Ben knew he didn't have much time. He scribbled a note and began making his way towards them, being careful to stay hidden. He crept as close as he could to Marie and the children. He heard Louis-Charles asking Marie if they could hide and seek.

"Yes, but don't go too far. I'll cover my eyes first and then you two hide." Marie began counting slowly to ten, "one, two, three..." As soon as the children ran off, Ben crept right up to her, pulled the rosary out of his pocket, and placed it along with the note near her feet. As he stole back to his hiding place, Marie commented, "I hear you! You better run and hide, I'm almost to ten."

When she opened her eyes, she looked all around and finally took off running towards some giggles she heard in the distance. Ben's heart sank. She did not see the note. His spirits were lifted when the trio came running back to where they started. The three of them were laughing, and as Marie Thérèse was about to count, Louis Charles almost stepped on the note. "Look!" he exclaimed. He handed the rosary and the note to his mother.

Ben watched Marie's reaction carefully as she clutched the rosary and read the note. She caught her breath, crumpling the paper in her hand. "What does it say Maman?"

"Oh, it's nothing my little man. Now hurry off and hide while your sister counts." As soon as he turned, she put the rosary around her neck and tucked it under the collar of her dress. Ben watched her face as she searched the forest. As hard as it was, he remained silent and hidden. He knew it wasn't time... not yet.

Chapter 44

As Marie Thérèse closed her eyes and counted, Marie spun in circles, searching the woods frantically, looking in all directions, but Ben remained hidden. Before Marie Thérèse could finish counting, Louis called for them, telling them all was ready to continue their journey. On the walk back to the carriage, Marie continued scanning the forest. As they boarded the coach, Louis Charles spoke up, "Papa, I found a treasure in the forest." Louis glanced back at Marie and she shrugged saying, "It was nothing, just rubbish."

"Well, we should be off then."

"Yes. Come along children, climb inside." Marie's hand clutched the side of the coach doorway. She paused, hesitating as she glanced back.

"Marie?"

"I'm coming," she whispered, as she boarded the coach. Her head was whirling as the coach started off again. She looked out her window, continuing her search. She gripped the note, tightly concealing it in the palm of her hand. She was desperate to reread it, but didn't dare. She went back over its contents in her mind...

Marie,

It's Ben. I hope you can remember the times we had together, as well as your fate. You are in grave danger. I am near you, and will try to help you as soon as I can. Whatever you do, do not go into Varennes.

Watch for me.
Forever... Ben

Now she knew. Her recent dreams were a sign, her subconscious trying to communicate with her heart. Faced with the actual concreteness of the note, and her rosary, she now realized the truth. Her time with Ben raced through her mind like wildfire. Meeting him at the Louvre, times they spent together in the apartment, as well as shopping, sharing meals, even sharing the same bed. The floodgates of her mind opened, and she knew they would never be closed again. She finally remembered...

Her forehead pressed against the carriage window, she smiled to herself, reminiscing just for a bit. As her mind marched through the days of her past, she remembered arriving back in time to Versailles, alone and confused. As her knowledge of the future began to surface, realization took hold... they would all be caught. They would be taken back to Paris, where in a few months Louis would die, she would die, and then sweet Louis Charles would die alone, in prison, after being horribly mistreated. Only her daughter would be spared, to live out her life, sad and lonely. Now focused on the survival of her family, she had no time to think of her love for Ben. She casually asked Louis how far it was to the next town.

"It will take all day," he answered. This was the longest part of their journey without a scheduled stop. She doubted Ben would have this information. *Is he following us? Has he gone on ahead?* She had no way of knowing. For hours she kept watch, hoping for a glimpse of him. With each passing mile the town of Varennes drew closer and closer, and her fear mounted.

Where is he? Why doesn't he show himself to me? She knew only one thing for certain. She would not leave her children behind. Her love for them was all that kept her going. They were caring, tender, warmhearted children. No matter what happened, they didn't deserve the harsh treatment that Marie knew awaited them. Her body shuddered when she thought of the horrible things Louis Charles would face—abuse, isolation, unspeakable brutality, and ultimately, dying alone. Was this truly their fate? She couldn't be sure, but she wouldn't take a chance. No, the only choice was to keep them with her no matter what.

What must Ben think, she wondered. He had met her when she was a young woman of 18. She had aged, and not aged well. *I look so old now, so unkempt. What about the children? Will he rescue them too? What does he know about the years since we last saw one another? Where has he been all this time?* She tried to put it all together, but could not. *He couldn't have been here long, or he would've come for me sooner.* He was willing to put his life on the line for her, she was sure of it, but what about Louis and the children?

Just after four o'clock, the carriage slowed as they passed through a tiny hamlet, where much to their dismay, many in the town knew who they were, and walked along as the carriage passed, happy to get a glimpse of their king. The violence of Paris had not reached the distant country towns and the people seemed pleased to see the royal couple. Recognition was something they needed to avoid. Obviously, the word was out.

Marie kept her eyes peeled for a glimpse of Ben, but never saw him. They made it through the town without mishap, but their apprehension grew. The children were now quiet, feeling the heaviness in the air. It was on the outskirts of this town that troops were supposed to be assembled and waiting to escort them safely to their ultimate destination. Marie turned to Louis, "How will our passage remain a secret, if so many know who we are?"

Louis patted the sweat from his forehead with a lace handkerchief, expertly monogrammed with his initials and crest. "I don't know. I didn't think this was a good idea, and now..." He glanced over at the children and gave them a weak smile.

Marie's mind screamed, *Louis is no help! Where was Ben? When will he show himself? What if something has happened to him?*

The carriage came to a stop about a mile out of town. They would wait for the arrival of the promised royal military escort, their protection for the rest of the journey.

Chapter 45

Ben watched as the carriage drove out of sight. He had seen the look on Marie's face, that moment of recognition. It gave him hope that her memory was coming back. It was all he could do not to come out of concealment, grab her hand, and flee.

He came up with a plan, and began following the carriage at a safe distance. Before long, Ben carefully took a side trail, hoping it would lead him past the carriage, and back out onto the road. The trail led just as he had hoped. Once back out on the open road, he pushed his horse hard, trying to put as much time and distance as possible between them.

He took out the map where Pierre had marked Chalons, the town the military escort was to meet the king and his family, and get them safely through Varennes, and then on to the border. As Ben rode through the small village, he didn't see anything unusual. There was no sign of an army anywhere. Now he knew he was truly their only hope.

He tied his horse to a tree, and walked to a small tavern in the center of town. He inquired where he might buy a horse. The proprietor shrugged, but another man spoke up and sent Ben to a large home on the west side of town. Once Ben had completed negotiations for the horse, he went back to the tree, and tied the two horses together.

Ben thought uneasily of Louis and the rest of the party, but pushed these thoughts from his mind. There was no way to save them all. Escaping with Marie and the children was the best he could hope for, and he wasn't sure if that could be accomplished or not.

But where will we go? Should we try to make it to the border? How risky would that be? Ben had no way of knowing. *Even more risky would be trying to get back to Versailles, to step through the door and try to get back home. Even if the door is a pathway to another time, I don't know where we would end up*. Ben pulled a leaf from a low hanging branch and absentmindedly peeled it apart. *But we must get out of the country, out of the present time. To stay here will be certain death.*

As Ben weighed the options, he realized they had no guarantees no matter what they chose. *Perhaps by some miracle we will make it back. It's a chance we'll have to take*. Obviously, they would have to get to Versailles as fast as possible. Once her disappearance was discovered, the entire country would be searched. No stone would be left unturned. *At least*, thought Ben, *I haven't seen or heard from Robespierre since I left him. Hopefully we'll be long gone before he gets word that Marie and the children are missing*. Ben felt sure Robespierre would be able to piece together their plan, and would try to stop them if he had any warning. He was hell bent on the demise of the royal family, and Marie in particular.

Ben sat and waited. Half an hour had passed by the time the cumbersome carriage came into view. He realized what a debacle this entire escape attempt actually was. The shiny new carriage must be causing a stir in each village they passed through. He knew they were in disguise, but still... simpler would've been better.

The coach rolled to a stop just outside of town, right across from where Ben was waiting. His nerves were on edge as he wondered how he would separate Marie and the children from the rest of the party.

As the sun dipped closer to the horizon, Ben moved in, but remained concealed among the trees. He overheard the conversation Louis had with the driver. They would stay put and wait for the protection of the army that was sure to arrive at any moment. Ben knew this would be his only chance.

When Marie and the children exited the coach, he saw her look around anxiously. *Just relax*, he thought, *I'm here*. His heart caught in his throat as he saw her looking scared and desperate, although it was obvious she was trying to conceal her feelings. The rest of the group decided to walk into town for a bit of food. Once they were gone, it was just Louis, Marie and the children. She spread a blanket out on the ground, and told the children to sit down and play quietly while they waited for their supper. She placed a few toy soldiers in front of Louis Charles, and gave Marie Thérèse some drawing pencils and a tablet. Louis reclined on the blanket and stretched out his legs. The last of the sunlight peeked through the tree leaves, right into his eyes, so he placed his hat over his face.

Before long, Marie told Louis she wanted to take a quick walk to stretch her legs. Without removing his hat, he told her to stay close and come back quickly. *She's trying to find me*, thought Ben. Going to the other side of the carriage, she made a quick decision. Instead of walking along the road, she headed straight into the woods. As soon as she was out of direct sight of the carriage, he came out into the open. Her back to him, he quietly whispered her name. She turned, and before he knew what happened, she was in his arms. Despite their desperate situation, fear melted away as they clung to one another. They spoke in hushed, but hurried tones.

"I can't believe it's you. You're here! Where have you been all these years?"

"What do you mean, it's only been a few days," said Ben.

"No, it hasn't. When I stepped through the door just before you, I entered my life just as I left it, back into 1773. I've been living my life here for the past 18 years."

Ben replied, "When I stepped through the door behind you, I entered into the present, only a week ago. I've been trying to get to you ever since. I saw you at the Tuileries, and you didn't know me."

"I saw you, but I didn't know who you were, I didn't remember anything. But now... I remember it all." Happy tears streamed down her face and as she spoke. Ben stroked her hair lovingly... but the mood changed quickly. They were both thrown back into their immediate situation. "What are we going to do now?"

"I have a plan. You and the children must come with me immediately. I've got two horses tied in a clearing just beyond this spot. The others have gone into town, and Louis isn't paying attention. It's our only chance."

Marie gasped, "What? Do you mean for me to leave Louis and the others behind?"

"It's the only way. There is no chance of us escaping with all of your family; we'll be found out, caught for sure." Marie shook her head no. Ben thought fast. "Perhaps if Louis delays the journey looking for you, it will save their lives. They may not go on to Varennes tonight as planned, and maybe, that will save them all!"

"I can't leave like this, knowing what will happen to Louis if he's caught. I must warn him, say goodbye to him! He won't understand!" She sobbed, suddenly overwhelmed with the choice she was being forced to make.

"Please Marie, there is no time to waste. Think of the children. Don't you remember the horrible things you read? The events to take place?" Marie nodded. Ben knew it was difficult for her to hear, but it was all he could think of to convince her. He knew her love for her children would prevail.

With just a moment's thought, Marie realized Ben was right. As much as she hated leaving the others behind, this was truly her children's only chance of survival, the only way. "I must warn Louis somehow. Please Ben, think of something."

He grabbed his canvas bag and tore off a corner of the map. He scribbled a note:

Do not enter Varennes.

"Here, place this note in the carriage. Gather the children, and if Louis asks, tell him you are taking the kids to show them something. Tell him you saw a rabbit or a bird's nest, anything. Start heading this way, and come back here to this spot. I will walk the horses over, and we'll be off."

"But where are we going?"

"Right now, the most important thing is to get as far away from here as possible. Now go! Be quick!" He did not tell her he had made the decision that they would be returning to Versailles. He wasn't sure how she would react, and there was no time to discuss it now.

Marie had only taken a few steps towards the carriage when they heard the sound of horses approaching fast. Ben grabbed her and they crouched down and hid out of sight. To their horror, it was Robespierre and an army of soldiers. They surrounded the carriage before Louis could react, and immediately seized him and the children at gunpoint. Confusion and shouting ensued. Marie tried to jump up but Ben held her back cupping his hand over her mouth. She fought him frantically. Finally, their eyes met and instantly she understood. They had no choice. They had to leave, NOW. There was no chance to save anyone. Marie felt helpless as she and Ben made their way to the horses tied to a tree about 50 yards deeper into the woods. So distraught, she was in no condition to handle a horse, so they climbed on together and rode out of sight, leaving the other horse behind.

"I wonder if they will try and follow?" Marie asked anxiously a few minutes later.

"I don't know. I don't think they saw us."

"Where exactly are we going? I mean, shouldn't we wait, remain hidden somewhere in the forest, until we can get back to the children?"

"We can't stop. They will begin searching as soon as they realize you are gone. They will find us if we stop anywhere near here. Trust me, it's the only way."

The pair rode on. They didn't dare travel on the road, afraid of discovery, instead they opted to stay in the forest. They had no idea what Robespierre and Louis would make of Marie's disappearance. No one would know she was with Ben. That in and of itself would give them a head start. No one would imagine she was on a horse headed west towards Paris. Ben could only imagine the scene back at the carriage. He couldn't even fathom what Marie must be feeling now. The only thing to do was to press on—press on to freedom and to life.

Chapter 46

"I will not ask you again, where is she?" shouted Robespierre. Louis remained silent. "Guards, put the king and the children into the carriage and do not let them out of your sight." He pointed to the guards. "The four of you fan out on both sides of the road and into the woods. The rest of you go into town. The coachmen must be there, perhaps getting food. Marie may be in town as well. All of you go, now! Do not return without the queen!"

Confused, Louis followed orders and climbed into the carriage with the children. Visibly shaken, they whispered the question on everyone's mind, "Papa, where is Maman?"

"I'm not sure. She went for a walk. Perhaps she saw them coming, and she's hiding somewhere."

"Has she left us?" asked Louis Charles, his bottom lip quivering.

"Of course not. She would never leave us. Be patient. She will be back." But as Louis said the words, he wasn't so sure. If she had a chance to escape, would she take it? *No, she would never leave the children,* he thought. *Maybe me, but not the children.*

Time passed. Soon the searchers returned with the coachmen and Louis' sister. The other searchers returned empty-handed. Robespierre was enraged. He couldn't believe it. He knew Ben had something to do with Marie vanishing. He would find them if it was the last thing he did.

He spoke to the captain of the guard. "Leave me six of your men. You and the rest of your soldiers return the king and his party to Paris. Go straight to the Tuileries. This time, surround every inch of the palace with guards, and have armed guards at the doors to their living quarters around the clock. They are all under arrest for the crime of treason against the French Republic. If any of them escape, it's to the guillotine with all of you."

The long journey back to Paris soon began, with the carriage completely surrounded by soldiers. Everyone inside shook with fear, except the children. Not understanding the full implications of being taken back to prison, they were not afraid. Instead they cried out in agony for their mother. Louis tried to console them, but to no avail. He continuously watched out the window, staring into the darkness, hoping for a glimpse of Marie.

As soon as the carriage rolled out of sight and Robespierre was satisfied Louis was secure, he turned to the six soldiers awaiting his orders. "I want two of you to continue on this road. Ride all the way to the border. Whatever you do, if you see Antoinette, do not let her cross over. Capture her and bring her directly to Paris. The reward for her capture will most definitely make it worth your while, but I want her back alive.

"The rest of you fan out on either side of the road and search the woods again. She couldn't have gone far. It's dark and she doesn't know these woods." As they turned to go he said, "One more thing. She might be traveling with a young man, so keep your eyes out for both of them. They may be in disguise. Search every house and farm within 20 miles of here."

"But where will you go?" asked one of the soldiers.

"I have my own idea of where she may be headed, but I cannot be sure. I will travel alone. It will be faster. If you find her and return her to Paris, I will find out in due time." With that, he turned his horse, and headed back down the road towards Paris, soon coming upon the carriage carrying Louis and the others. He smiled and licked his lips as he passed. He was returning to Versailles. Ben and Marie were headed there; he felt it in his gut. He must get there first and prevent them from trying to escape through the door.

Chapter 47

The farther Marie and Ben traveled away from her family, the more agitated she became. She had to find a way to rescue her children, but how? Traveling in the dark was slow, but luck was on their side. There was a full moon to light their way. After traveling quite a distance, the horse tired. They stopped and dismounted. "We'll take a few minutes and give him time to rest. Let's sit down and rest as well." Marie said nothing, but did as she was told. Ben decided to keep the conversation to a minimum, knowing she was coping with the grisly scene they had left behind.

"Perhaps you should try and close your eyes for a few minutes. I'll keep watch."

The pressure was too much. Suddenly Marie snapped. "Keep watch? Keep watch! Yes Ben, you must keep watch over the precious queen. But who's keeping watch over my children?"

"I'm so sorry Marie... I didn't mean..."

"Sorry? You should be sorry. Now you've separated me from the most important people in my life."

"But you saw what happened. There was no time. Would sacrificing yourself have saved them?"

"I don't know, maybe." She turned away from him. It broke his heart.

"Listen to me. Everything has changed now. If I hadn't found you, history would repeat itself. You would be caught, returned to Paris, and eventually sent to the guillotine. At least this way, our actions have changed any probability that events will happen in the same way. They will search for you, they won't find you, and that will change everything. There is no way of knowing if the king will even lose his life. Everything is different now. We have altered the future."

Marie clung to his words. *Maybe he's right! Everything* has *changed. Maybe Louis and the children will live. Maybe there is hope!* He had not just saved her, but by showing up, his presence had possibly saved them all.

"You still haven't told me where we are going. We seem to be heading back toward Paris."

"Yes, in that general direction." Ben chose his next words carefully. "I've been thinking... there is no way to hide you in France. You will eventually be recognized, found out. If we take you to another country, who knows what will happen? They might return you to France, and even if they don't, you will always be in fear for your life, constantly looking over your shoulder. We know Robespierre wishes you dead, and will not rest until that happens." Ben took a deep breath. "My thought is, we should return to Versailles, to your bedroom, and go through the door."

"It won't work. I tried and tried it when I first came back. It never worked."

"But I was just there a week ago, and the pathway was open. The door brought me here, to your time. Perhaps it will take us forward, back to mine."

"But that would mean me leaving my children forever."

"Don't you think they would want you to escape, to live?"

"I think all they want right now is their mother. I can't imagine how they feel, other than abandoned."

"But they aren't abandoned. They have their father."

Marie sat in silence as she realized that yes, they had their father, and he loved them very, very much. He would do everything in his power to save them, to protect them. Her fears began to subside just a bit.

They sat in silence for a long time. Finally, Ben could stand it no longer. He had to ask her the question that had been burning in his heart. "I have to ask you something. How did you forget me? What happened?"

"I'm not exactly sure. Now, thinking back, I remember being completely distraught over losing you and returning to my old life. I remember not eating, or drinking, and finally Louis had the chemist mix up some sort of tonic for me. I had a severe reaction to the solution, and when I recovered, my memories of you and of the future were all gone. It wasn't until I saw you outside the palace fence at the Tuileries that it all began coming back to me."

"All of it?"

"Not at first. I started having very vivid dreams. You kept coming to me, but would disappear before we could speak. Then in the woods earlier, when I saw the rosary and the note in your handwriting, everything came rushing back. And yes, I remem-

ber all of it now." She moved over closer to him, and he took her in his arms. As soon as they kissed, an overwhelming desire came over her. She felt her passions rekindled for the first time since she was eighteen, and immediately she yearned for him. Her fears melted away as they lay down in the grass together. Her desire was strong. The emotional exhaustion left her, and she had only one thought: Ben.

Every feeling they had rose to the surface. She not only allowed him to make love to her, she responded back, with passion. It felt foreign to her, but at the same time, it felt like she was coming home.

Once their lovemaking ended, they did not want to let go of one another, but they knew they had to go. They stood up and Marie turned away, suddenly shy and embarrassed as she adjusted her clothing. Without speaking, they both knew they would stay together no matter what. The bond was set. They climbed back on the horse, Ben at the reigns and Marie behind him. She locked her hands around his waist and whispered in his ear. "I don't think the doorway will work, but I'm willing to try, as long as I'm with you."

Chapter 48

They traveled all through the night and into the next day. Both were tired and hungry, but pressed on. By late afternoon heavy clouds and fog had moved in. The temperature dropped rapidly. Marie shivered as they rode through the now familiar woods. They were getting closer to their destination. Finally, the forest opened up, and through the fog they could just make out the Palace of Versailles in the distance. Their nerves began to intensify as they drew nearer to the chateau.

"I don't think it wise to approach on horseback. I think we need to walk the final distance. If Robespierre has figured out our plan, he may already be waiting." Ben took the bridle out of the horse's mouth, slapped his rear, and sent him on his way. They began the long walk along the man-made lakes to the palace, being careful to walk among the trees, not out in the open.

Finally, they stopped. They had worked their way to one end of the massive buildings. It didn't matter where they entered, Marie would be able to find her way to her bedroom. As Ben turned the handle and opened the massive door near the L'Orangerie area, it creaked loudly. They froze. Finally, not hearing any other sounds, they let out their breath, and stepped inside.

The sun had set, and a light mist began to fall. They would have to find their way through the enormous building in the dark. There were no candles lit anywhere.

As they carefully made their way through the halls and their eyes adjusted to the lack of light, Marie could not believe the condition of her former home. The destruction was everywhere, broken glass, shattered mirrors, slashed paintings. All the symbols of royalty and her old way of life were destroyed. Tears filled her eyes when she saw the beauty of the chateau treated as if it were worthless. She quickened her step, wanting to get to the bedroom and escape. If the people of France were willing to destroy such beauty for sport, what would they be willing to do to her? Then her children's faces flashed across her mind, and immediately she shoved those images aside. *They are with their father. He will be able to save them.*

As they crept along, Ben imagined what Marie must be feeling. Images of her past life had to be going through her mind. *We must go quickly. She may change her mind... not want to leave.*

They walked on, turning each corner carefully. At last they reached the center wing where the bedroom was located, their hearts beating with anticipation. When they reached the long hall that would lead directly to her room, to their horror, they saw the glow of candlelight just beyond the door. Immediately they backtracked a bit and hid in a small gallery off to one side. Marie whispered, "Do you think it's him?"

"It has to be. The rest of the chateau seems deserted. The only light is coming from your bedroom. He's figured out our

plan, but he has no way of knowing I'm with you. He must have headed here as soon as he left Louis."

"I wonder if he's alone?"

"I don't know. You stay here, I'll go see and be right back."

"No! Please don't leave me. We cannot be separated again!"

"I promise... I'll be right back. I just want to see if he's alone."

"No... don't go," she said, as he took off his boots and began walking barefoot back down the long hall. She felt desperate to follow him as she watched his silhouette disappear into the darkness, but decided to do as he asked. Perspiration dripped down her back in the heavy, cumbersome dress she wore. It was hot and humid in the cavernous building with no air movement of any kind.

Time passed slowly. She was too far away to hear anything through the heavy door of the gallery. After waiting patiently for some time, she could stand it no longer. She tiptoed over to the door, opened it slowly, and peered down the hall. Staring into the darkness her eyes went in and out of focus. She thought she saw a figure approaching, but then, nothing. She cautiously began making her way to the bedroom. She had to find out what had happened to Ben.

Marie crept silently down the corridor, with each step getting closer and closer to the eerie glow of the candlelight. Halfway there she froze mid-step, sensing something just behind her. The hair on her neck stood straight up, and instantly she began running the rest of the way. Just before getting to the doorway of the room, she was grabbed from behind. "Well, well, well, who have we here?"

"Let me go!"

"Not on your life Antoinette. Ben has been caught. He told me he had no idea where you were. I knew better. Let's go see him, shall we?"

They entered the bedroom and near the doorway to the dressing room stood Ben, pinned to the wall by a gun held to his chest by an unknown man. Swallowing hard, Marie looked into Ben's eyes and mouthed, "I'm sorry."

"So, you thought you could get back to the future together, didn't you? I'm here to make sure that doesn't happen. In fact, I believe we'll send Ben back alone. You can watch him go on to freedom, and you, well, you know what's going to happen to you, don't you Antoinette?"

"No, I won't leave without her," said Ben through clenched teeth.

"Either you go through the door, or I'll kill her here, right now, on the spot. Now go!" The other man stared at Robespierre, not understanding a word of what was being said about the door, the future—any of it. Robespierre nodded for him to force Ben through the door. He jabbed Ben a few times in the chest with the gun, but Ben stood firm.

Running out of patience, and ready for Ben to be out of the picture, Robespierre grabbed the gun and ordered his friend to hold on to Marie. "Put a knife to her throat," he said, as he reached in his coat pocket and tossed one over. "Now go through the door Ben, or she's dead."

"Go Ben... save yourself... it's what must be."

"I won't leave you."

"Slit her throat!" yelled Robespierre.

"Stop! I'll go. I'll go. But remember," Ben turned to the man holding the knife against Marie's neck and said, "this man is a murderer and a liar. You should not listen to him. You should fear him. He might try and send Marie to the guillotine, he might even send you, but guess what?" He turned to Robespierre. "You should have read the history books when you had the chance. You will die by the guillotine as well."

As soon as Ben finished speaking, the man holding Marie was in such shock, that his hand fell to his side. Robespierre, in shock as well, let his guard down for just a moment. When he did, Ben yelled to Marie, "Run!"

She was one step ahead of him when she stepped through the doorway. As Ben was about to step through, Robespierre managed to grab his arm. Ben jerked forward, the grasp slipped, and Robespierre fell backwards onto the ground. As Ben stepped over the threshold, he grabbed the door and slammed it shut, breaking it off its hinges. It crashed loudly to the floor.

Immediately, all was quiet and still. The two men left behind, stood silently, staring at the doorway where they had both just seen two people disappear into thin air. Then Robespierre spoke, "I won't go to the guillotine, I won't." He walked over to the dressing room, paused, turned to his friend and said, "Goodbye." He then stepped through the doorway.

He stood on the other side for a moment and then turned around. He was still in the same spot. He stepped back and forth through the doorway, over and over, and nothing happened. The gateway had closed. He would go nowhere. He would have to stay, with the knowledge of his impending death.

As reality set in, he slowly fell to his knees, crying and beating his fists on the ground. His friend stood next to him, not knowing what to say or do.

Chapter 49

Present Day

Diana hung up the phone in exasperation. Once again, her brother Ben did not answer. She had repeatedly left messages, but he had not returned any of her calls. She had wanted to talk to him about Marie, hoping to glean a little more insight into the nature of their relationship. Her reason for calling had been frivolous, but now she was beginning to get concerned. It was not like him to ignore her calls. She checked in with her father, and casually asked if he had heard from Ben lately. He hadn't, but not wanting to worry him, she laughed it off, telling her father he was probably busy with work.

Another few days went by with no word. Late that afternoon she called the hospital where he worked. When she asked to speak to Ben, the call was immediately transferred to the head of the department. Diana was informed that Ben had not reported to work in over a week. They had called him repeatedly and even gone to his apartment, but he was nowhere to be found. Ben's superior had hoped Diana could shed some light on his whereabouts, and was surprised that she had not heard from her brother either. She thanked him, hung up the phone and immediately called to book a flight from London to Paris. At this late hour only one flight remained, and it was full.

She immediately went to her computer and booked a seat on the next available train to Paris, leaving at 9:00 p.m. As she packed a small suitcase, she realized she had no idea what she would do to find him. Her first thought was to head straight to the apartment and ask his neighbors if they had seen or heard anything unusual. If nothing materialized from that, she would have to call the police and report him missing. Maybe she was overreacting, but *better safe than sorry*, she thought. Within the hour, she was comfortably seated on the Eurostar train to Paris.

At midnight she stood in front of his door, fumbling in her purse for the spare key Ben had given her. She took a deep breath as she turned the key in the lock and opened the door. Her heart sank; the apartment was empty. She called out to him, but was met with silence. She looked around for clues, but she saw nothing unusual, or out of place. In the bathroom, she noticed Marie's toiletries on the counter, and her robe hanging on the hook on the door. *So, Marie is still staying with Ben. But where are they?*

She walked back into the den, and noticed a pink journal embossed with gold filigree on the desk. She opened it, and written inside the cover in ornate handwriting were the words, *Marie Antoinette*. At that moment, an invisible force seemed to move through Diana's body. She felt the ground shake beneath her feet, the pages of the diary fluttered, but she gripped it tightly. At the same time, a book fell to the floor from the bookshelf behind her.

What she didn't know, was at that exact same moment, Marie had stepped through the door in Versailles. Simultaneously, all the books that referenced Marie Antoinette and the French Revolution, mysteriously fell from bookshelves all over the world. The only account of the time travel was the diary—the diary clutched in Diana's hand, which kept her connected to the true story.

An ominous feeling came over her as she sat down on the couch and opened the journal, hoping to gain some information she could use to find Ben. The story she read was incomprehensible. She could not put it down. The last entry was dated over a week ago, and stated that Marie wished to return to Versailles, but that Ben was against it.

Diana sat back in shock. The journal was intimate. It was a story of falling in love, a story of complete fantasy, but somehow, it seemed real.

She needed to refresh herself on Marie Antoinette's story. She walked over to the large bookshelf, and saw Ben's history book on the floor. It was opened to the section on the French Revolution. To Diana's shock, the story was not as she remembered. In this version, Marie had mysteriously disappeared and was never found.

What in the world? Diana could not make sense of the changes in the book. Her spirit felt odd, like something was happening all around her. She felt compelled to go out on the balcony.

Standing in the dark and looking out over the city of Paris, she heard rolling thunder in the distance. Other than that, the city looked normal, but she didn't feel normal. *What is happening to me? Am I going crazy? Are my thoughts playing tricks on me in my desperation?* She closed the balcony doors and returned to the diary, rereading every word in earnest. *This is crazy*, thought Diana, *there is no way Marie Antoinette was here, with Ben.* Then she thought back to the strange way Ben and Marie had acted when she surprised them with the visit, and how evasive Ben was when speaking of Marie at their dinner the following night.

It was late. Diana decided to stay at the apartment for the night. If Ben didn't show up by morning, she would alert the authorities.

Chapter 50

Marie tumbled into the darkness. "Ben?" There was no sound, no answer. "It can't be! Not again!" She jumped up and walked over to the window of her bedroom and jerked the heavy drapes open. The moon was full and light flooded the room. The bedroom was no longer in shambles, it was in order, but it was quite empty. Only her bed stood behind the golden railing. The paintings on the wall had changed again. Immediately she knew she had made it back to the future. *But where is Ben? He was with me. We stepped through the door together. I felt his presence just behind me.* She walked back over to the dressing room doorway and looked through it, careful not to lean into the space. She saw no sign of Ben. She waited.

After what seemed like an eternity, she went over to her bed to sit down, keeping her eyes continuously on the doorway, willing Ben to come back to her. Over time, the possibility hit her hard, the possibility that he would not come. Tears streamed down her face as she realized she was completely alone in the world. In a matter of 24 hours she had lost her husband, her children, and now Ben.

Wait! she thought, *maybe he entered time on the calendar before me. Maybe he's waiting for me at the apartment, or looking for me in Paris! He could also have entered time after me. Maybe*

I should go to the apartment and wait for him to find me. She knew, of course, that he could be years apart from her, as had happened before. There was also the dreadful prospect that he was left behind in 1791.

I'll wait the rest of the night, and then if he's not back by morning, I'll go to Paris and wait there. She remembered the green building she had visited back when she was here the first time. Not feeling nearly as frightened as before, she made her way to the back gardens of the palace. As she walked, a light mist began to float through the air like fine particles of dust. She went across the vast grounds in the dark, and managed to find the green building without any trouble. She tried to open the same door, but this time, it was locked. She jiggled the door, nothing. Finally, she rammed her shoulder into it as hard as she could. The flimsy lock gave way and she was inside.

She pushed the button on the top of the cash register, it opened with a ding, but to her shock, it was empty. There was no money inside the drawer. *Now, how will I get the train to Paris?* Disappointed she turned to leave, and a metal box stored on a shelf under the cash register caught her eye. Bending down, she grabbed it, unlatched the lid, and inside she found a few wadded up bills and some coins. She gathered all of it in her fist, and quickly returned to the bedroom. Once there, she spread the money out, but it was too dark to see. Thinking back all those years ago, she remembered Ben flipping on and off the light switches in the apartment. She walked over to the doorway, and sure enough, there was a panel of light switches just to the left. She flipped one of them up, and suddenly her room was flooded with light. She counted out 17 euro, plenty of cash for a train ticket back to Paris. She decided to stay the night, and leave early in the morning, always aware that Ben could come crashing through the doorway at any second. Finally, she fell into a restless sleep.

As soon as the sun rose, Marie made her way out of the palace and hid off to the side of the carriage house. Once she saw the front gates open, and the courtyard begin to fill with people, she made her way quickly to the train station. Keeping her head down, she knew she looked a fright. Her ornate dress was filthy, she smelled of horses, and her hair was a complete mess. At least she had thought to take off her wig and tuck it under the bed back at the palace.

Once at the train station, she immediately made her way to the restroom and tidied herself up as best as she could. She took a mound of paper towels and washed her arms, hands and feet. She splashed her face with cold water and smoothed her hair.

Returning to the sales window, she purchased a ticket and quickly boarded the next train to Paris. She sat on the back row, trying to act nonchalant, ignoring the stares she got from tourist and locals alike. Parisians were pretty accepting of anything and anybody, no matter how strange, so no one questioned her. Perhaps they thought she was an actor in a play, going to rehearsal in her wide hooped dress, tight corset, and long, bell-shaped lace sleeves reaching down to her fingertips.

Once the train pulled into the Notre Dame station, she disembarked and began making her way through the crowded streets. On her way to the apartment, it never occurred to her to find out the year. She assumed it was as before. There was only one thing on her mind—to find Ben.

Chapter 51

When Marie saw the apartment building in the distance, she quickened her step. *He's here. I just know it!* She took the stairs two at a time, almost tripping over the heaviness of her dress. She stood before his door, prayed a silent prayer, and then, she knocked.

Seconds later she heard someone coming. She couldn't believe it! When the door opened and she saw Diana standing there, her heart sank. "Please tell me he's here."

"He isn't. Who are you?"

"I'm Marie. Remember?"

Diana squinted her eyes, barely seeing the resemblance to the young Marie she had met just two weeks ago. "I don't understand. You can't be her. She was much younger."

"Ben isn't here? Have you seen him?"

"No," was all Diana could say in her confusion. Marie glanced over her shoulder into the apartment, and noticed her pink diary open on the dining table.

"We need to talk. You've got to help me."

"Yes, I agree," said Diana, and held the door open for Marie to pass.

Diana made a kettle of hot tea, and the two of them sat down for what would turn out to be a lengthy conversation lasting late into the afternoon. By the end of it, Diana was full of doubts and questions, but deep down inside, the story was so intricate and so detailed, that she knew in her heart Marie was for real and was telling the truth, but the more pressing question remained... what now?

In the end, they decided the best thing to do was wait. They could not alert the police, talk to the family, or to the neighbors. They knew no one would believe them. They were on their own and vowed to stay together until they found Ben, or discovered what had happened to him.

That evening, Marie took a long, hot bath. Despite the grim circumstances, washing her hair and body felt luxurious. Diana wanted to help her in any way she could, so when Marie emerged from the bathroom, she gave her some scented lotion for her skin, and offered to fix her hair and apply some makeup she had brought with her from London. Not only was Diana current with all the latest fashion, she was quite skillful with makeup and only used the best French brands.

Marie's distress lightened a bit as she sat still for her makeover. Before long the bathroom counter resembled a full-service salon, and the two women seemed more like sisters than strangers who were just getting to know one another. Once Diana was finished, Marie turned and looked in the mirror, and suddenly broke out into tears.

"Don't cry, your mascara will run," said Diana, laughing as she watched Marie stare at herself in the mirror. She had not seen herself look so young and beautiful in many years. The makeup and hairstyle gave her back the youthful appearance she had as a teen.

Marie went over to the closet and carefully hung up her filthy dress and petticoats. She then pulled out one of the dresses she had bought on her shopping spree with Ben. It seemed an eternity ago to her, yet the dress smelled fresh and felt soft between her fingers. She walked into the living area where Diana sat. "You look absolutely stunning."

"Thank you so much. I wish Ben could see me now."

At that moment, a key turned in the lock, the apartment door opened, and Ben walked into the room. Marie and Diana screamed and ran to him, all three embracing, laughing, and crying at the same time. Ben had stepped into the future timeline just hours after Marie caught the train to Paris. Now as he looked at the beautiful young woman before him, he was overcome with emotion and thankfulness. Their ordeal was over. They were safe, together, and would remain that way, forever.

Chapter 52

1791

The trip back to Paris was ominous. Louis was now relieved they had not found Marie. Perhaps she had a chance of survival. Perhaps she would make it across the border and strike a deal to secure Louis and the children's release. Maybe she could help restore the monarchy from a distance with the help of Austria. At this point, his wife was his only hope.

Once back in Paris, Louis and the children were returned to the Tuileries, where they received harsher treatment than before. All respect for his position had been lost. Now he was not only known as a deserter of his country, but many believed he knew of Marie's whereabouts. Louis was interrogated every day while men from the revolutionary army searched the countryside at a furious pace. A date was soon set. His trial was imminent.

Louis had nightmares about his missing wife. Various scenarios played out in his mind night after night. He was now completely alone. Without his beloved wife to lean on, he spent most of his days completely despondent, and without hope.

Eventually, the political climate in the city grew worse, and Louis was moved to the Temple, a grisly prison housed in a medieval fortress in the middle of Paris. Here he would await his trial. The children remained together in the Tuileries.

Approximately six months after being brought back to Paris after the failed escape attempt, Louis was put to death in the center of Paris by guillotine.

Once Louis was beheaded, many thought things would calm down in France, but just the opposite happened. The king's death seemed to ratchet things to a fever pitch. Without a king to blame for all the ills of France, and the queen nowhere to be found, the revolutionaries began to turn on one another. The guillotine continued in daily use. No one was safe from death. Neighbor turned against neighbor, friend against friend. Fear hung in the air like a noose.

The search for Marie Antoinette continued. The reward for her return grew. Villages and towns were searched one by one, as well as the countryside, but there was no sign of her. Her disappearance was a mystery that refused to be solved.

Then one day a man came forward with an incredible story about Marie disappearing through a doorway in Versailles. Of course, no one believed him, but when Robespierre's name was inserted into the story, many became intrigued. Another man came forward with a letter he had received from Robespierre, claiming he had been to the future and had seen Marie Antoinette there.

As more and more pieces of the puzzle were put together, it became apparent that Robespierre had a connection to the queen's disappearance. His name was on the register at the Tuileries that he had visited Marie privately just a few days before the escape attempt, and he was the one who had found Louis and the children on the road to the border. It was determined that Robespierre had obviously helped Marie Antoinette escape. He was asked repeatedly where she was, but he claimed not to know. During his trial, he tried to claim his innocence, but the more he talked, the more they laughed at his outlandish stories. They deemed him mad and he was thrown into the Tower Prison at the Conciergerie. The following day, he was taken to the guillotine and beheaded, in exactly the same way he had previously condemned so many others.

The days of high-priced bread and hunger seemed mild compared to the Reign of Terror that continued for many more months. Blood was spilled daily. By the end of the revolution, estimates suggest that from 20,000 to 40,000 people lost their lives to the guillotine. At first the citizens seemed to enjoy the executions, but by the end, they had become numb to the killing. The people of France had lost their soul.

Epilogue

Five Years Later

Marie placed her teacup back on its saucer and wrapped her shawl closer around her body. The lights of Paris were just beginning to glow, her favorite time of the evening. She enjoyed sitting alone on the balcony at the end of a long day. This particular evening, she was feeling reflective, thinking back over the past five years.

She was remembering a cloudy spring morning, about 9 months after she and Ben had come forward to the present day. She had turned to him and said, "It's time."

"Today?"

"Yes, today." Marie loaded her pink handbag with her compact, lipstick, and cell phone.

"Okay, let's go." Ben and Marie rode down the elevator, walked through a beautifully appointed courtyard, and got into their blue Peugeot Coupe parked in the entryway of their luxury apartment building. Ben slid into the driver's seat, as always. Marie got in on the other side and buckled her seatbelt, checking it twice. She was willing to ride in the car, but never felt completely safe at the speed it traveled.

She had waited months and months to face this day, to finally close the book on the final chapter of her past. Driving from the center of Paris to St. Denis would take them approximately 20 minutes. She leaned against the side of the car door and closed her eyes thinking of those she held most dear.

When they had first come back to the present, it had been extremely difficult for her. Even though she felt safe and secure with Ben, she longed for her children. She knew in her head that they had now been dead for over 200 years, but in her lifetime, she had just lost them, and missed them terribly. There were times Ben wondered if she would ever recover. She cried herself to sleep too many nights to count, mourning their passing. She missed Louis as well. He was a good man with a good heart. He had been kind to her and although she never felt about him the way she feels about Ben, he had been a good father. He was simply not meant to lead France. Neither of them had had the luxury of choosing their lives for themselves. They simply did the best they could.

One night, a few weeks after they had returned to the present, Ben, unable to sleep, went into the other room to read. As he looked over the bookshelf, his eyes rested on his old French history book. He took it off the shelf sat down on the couch and began reading, feeling nervous about what it might reveal. He had not mentioned anything to Marie, but he constantly looked over his shoulder, not knowing if Robespierre would appear. Reading about the French Revolution, and seeing the changes to the story, gave him a sense of relief and closure. It was fascinating to read about Marie's disappearance, and the fact that she had never been found. He also found out the fate of Robespierre, and now knew he would never be back. He also learned the fate of Louis and the children.

The next morning, he had carefully broached the subject with Marie. He offered to tell her what had transpired in the years after they left 18th century France, but she had refused his offer, not ready to hear the reality of what had happened to her family. If they had suffered, she would never be able to forgive herself. She did want to know about Robespierre, and was relieved they would never see him again.

Being thrust back into modern life had been overwhelming. There was so much to learn, so many details to remember. Ben was extremely patient with her, and explained things over and over until she understood. Sometimes he felt cheated, angry that they hadn't gotten to stay together when they first met. So many years lost, but he would wait. He knew she loved him and eventually the grief would lessen a bit, and maybe they could enjoy life again. He ached for her loss, and would have done anything to take the pain away.

Finally, nine months later, on that spring day, she felt ready to take the first step towards closure, ready to face the truth. Carefully Ben pulled the car into a parking spot at the Basilique Cathédrale de Saint-Denis, located in the northern suburbs of Paris. Ben had done research when Marie asked, and found out this church was the final resting place of King Louis XVI. Ben eyed her carefully as they walked up to the entrance of the massive medieval church. He was concerned for her.

They made their way slowly around the interior of the cathedral, Ben following Marie's lead. She stopped often and gazed at the plaques and memorials to many of the former Kings of France.

Finally, they came to it, the place where Louis had been laid to rest. Above his crypt, was a massive sculpture of him kneeling in prayer. The artist had truly captured Louis' likeness. Marie felt like she was staring into the eyes of the man himself. She read how he had died during the revolution by the guillotine. Marie knew this in her heart, although she had never sought out the information. Now the truth was right in front of her. Enough time had passed. She knelt near the statue and bowed her head, saying a silent prayer on his behalf.

She led Ben back out to the car, and once inside, she turned to him and said, "Thank you for understanding. I finally felt it was time to make peace with the past."

"Are you all right?"

"Yes, I'm fine."

"How about going out to lunch? We could go over to our favorite café on Île St. Louis."

"That would be lovely."

The sun had come out, so they took their seats at an outdoor table overlooking the Seine, and ordered a bottle of sparking water. Looking out over the river, Marie said, "I'm ready to learn more. I want to know the fate of my children."

"Here? Now?"

"Yes, Ben. I'm ready for you to tell me what you've found out."

"All right." Ben paused not sure where to start. "They made it out of France. Once Louis was killed, Robespierre began campaigning for the children to go to the guillotine as well. He pushed it too far. The people began turning against him. He went mad, telling everyone about the time travel. No one believed him of

course. He was sent to the guillotine, and soon after that, the children were released and escorted to Austria."

"Your sister Maria Carolina raised them. They led happy lives surrounded by their relatives. They both married, and Marie Thérèse had several children. They lived close to one another their entire lives. It all worked out, Marie. Marie Thérèse named her oldest daughter after you, calling her Antonia. You don't have to worry about them anymore. By leaving them, you ultimately saved them."

Relief followed by tears of joy streamed down Marie's face as Ben spoke. She couldn't believe what she was hearing, and now wished she had asked sooner, but she simply hadn't been ready. This was truly a happy day. Her children had both had long, happy, fulfilling lives. It was more than she dared hope for. She couldn't stop smiling.

That was the day Marie finally started looking forward– she finally accepted that she would never go back to her old life, never see her children or family again. Despite being hopelessly in love with Ben, this final step had been necessary for her to truly move forward.

The sun had set and the wind picked up, so Marie left the balcony and walked back into the bedroom. As she passed by her dressing table, she noticed her rosary glinting in the light. She was taken back again to the past, thinking about the early days just after their return. She and Ben had taken a lot of time deciding what they would do with their lives. He immediately went back to his job, never giving an explanation for his absence. About a month later, when he came in from work, Marie told him she had something to show him. She acted very mysterious as she walked into the bedroom.

She emerged with the dress and petticoats she had been wearing when she moved forward in time. Ben looked on as Marie began clipping threads and opening the folds of the undergarment. To Ben's shock, out spilled earrings, necklaces, rings, and gold coins. Marie chose a pair of earrings to keep, and then they slowly sold the rest of the pieces, sometimes consigning them to high-end auction houses, and other times they took them to the antique dealer who had originally assessed Marie's rosary. The owner had connections to private collectors all over the world, willing to pay top dollar for such ornate, historical pieces. Marie and Ben chose to remain anonymous as the pieces were sold one by one. They were both amazed at how easy the sales went, and it didn't take long to amass a small fortune.

They moved out of Ben's tiny place, and used the money to purchase a spacious apartment on the top floor of a chic 19th century Haussmann building in the 4th arrondissement. The apartment had been remodeled and modernized, but still had the charm and grace of the century when it was built. It still had three of the original fireplaces, wooden beams in the kitchen, and magnificent molding in every room. The dining room had an exquisite chandelier, and retained an original stone wall on one end. There were three nice-sized bedrooms with large French doors, each leading out to a private balcony. The apartment was just right for the two of them, and Marie's spirits lifted as they decorated their new home. Her passion for all things lovely was rekindled. She felt herself coming back to life as she chose fabrics, pillows, furniture, and artwork.

The only other person that knew the truth about Marie was Diana. The two of them became quite close, so much so that Diana left her life in London and moved to Paris. Soon a plan developed—a plan that would involve all three of them. They decided to open a small design business in the fashionable Le Marais district not far from the apartment. Ben devised a business plan, and took care of the financial side of the venture.

Diana's passion had always been in fashion, and of course Marie had an uncanny sense of fit, design, and fabrics. Their designs seamlessly married the styles from the past and the present. They worked extremely well together, and their small shop was soon bursting at the seams with ideas, patterns, textiles, and other materials. They named their company Regal Revolution, mixing modern and antique styles into a perfect French blend. They started off small, but were quickly noticed by a high-end designer in the city, and soon had more financial backing than they ever dreamed of.

They expanded their designs to include shoes, dresses, jewelry, purses and other accessories. Both women were in their element, and worked hard to be ready for their first showing at Paris fashion week the following fall. It was a lot of work, but they both found it more than rewarding and quite stimulating. Ben diligently worked behind the scenes as CEO. It was an exciting time for all of them.

Marie and Ben worked tirelessly during the day, but the evenings were all theirs. They grew closer every day. Neither one of them could imagine life without the other. One evening Ben took Marie out for an incredible dinner. During dessert, he surprised her with a beautiful engagement ring. She was moved beyond words, and the following month they were married in a simple ceremony, with Diana as witness. As they said their vows, her rosary dangled from her hand, just hidden by a bouquet of white roses. They had come full circle, and the future was theirs. They had nothing ahead of them, but time.

THE END

Author's Note

From the first moment I walked onto the grounds of Versailles, I felt an incredible connection to the past. It was as if I had been there before. Although I found the palace massive and on a scale I did not expect, it was the little details that caught my eye and touched my heart.

I will never forget walking up a grand staircase while holding onto the exquisite railing. My mind was focused on the beauty of my surroundings, when underfoot I felt a slight indentation. I crouched down and ran my hand over the smooth, cold stone. Time had worn away the stone ever so slightly right next to the handrail. A chill of realization went through my body. I was walking in the exact footsteps of those before me, and their shadow seemed to loom over my shoulder, asking me to understand their world, and see them as real people just like me.

Later, standing in Marie Antoinette's bedroom, I noted the intricacies of the décor. The room did not match the overall impression I had of her from the pages of history. It reminded me of a little girl's room, with delicate flowers embossed on the wallpaper and bedspread. From the top of the four golden bedposts stood large white feathers that brushed the ceiling. Exquisite embroidery detailed her initials, an intertwined M and A, right in the center of the headboard. Sadness came over me as I thought about her eventual end. I carried the experience in my heart as

I walked back to the train station to return to Paris. I determined then and there to find out all I could about this incredible place, and more importantly, about the people who lived there.

I would return many times over the next few years, each visit adding a layer to my understanding and fascination with royalty of the 18th century. The story of Louis XVI and Marie Antoinette, the last king and queen to occupy Versailles before the revolution, captivated me, but at the same time, the circumstances surrounding their deaths, haunted me.

Many people that read this book will wonder why I treated Marie with a level of sympathy and pity. The more I learned about her, the more I connected with the essence of who she really was, not the cliché she has become. It is impossible for us in the modern world to truly put ourselves in her shoes, and know how we would act under similar circumstances at such a young age.

I learned a lot about Marie and her family over the years through my personal visits to Versailles, the library, and online research. I found conflicts throughout. It was hard to pin down the absolute truth.

However, I found a treasure trove on information in historical writings, particularly the book, *Memoirs of the Court of Marie Antoinette Queen of France*, written by Madame Campan, the First Lady in Waiting to the Queen. She was present at Versailles when Marie Antoinette first arrived, and was a part of Marie's inner circle and was privy to all that transpired. If you would like to know more, this book can be found in its entirety online and is listed in the reference section at the end of this book.

What is it about Marie Antoinette that causes us to still speak of her hundreds of years after her death? What continues to draw people to her story? The more I learned throughout the years, the more I wanted Marie to live, to find true love and happiness. Obviously, this novel is a work of fiction, but parts of it are tied to true events. On the following pages, you will find a short summary of what really happened, and how my characters' real-life stories unfolded.

What Really Happened

Louis Charles

Louis Charles was born in 1785 in the palace Versailles as a royal prince, the third child of Louis and Marie. When his older brother died 4 years later, Louis Charles became the dauphin, next in line to the throne. He was only 6 years old when the Royal family was taken by force from their home and imprisoned in the Tuileries Palace in the center of Paris. He was with his family on the escape attempt when they were discovered and captured just 8 miles from the German border. They were escorted back to Paris, and eventually put into the Temple prison, which was housed in a medieval fortress within the city limits near the Conciergerie.

Once his father Louis XVI was executed, the nobles in exile recognized Louis Charles as the King of France. Soon he was separated from everyone he knew, torn from his mother's arms in the middle of the night despite her pleas and utter panic. From then on, he was kept in a separate area of the prison under the watchful eye of a cobbler named Antoine Simon, also a revolutionary, whose sole purpose was to cause Louis Charles to forget his royal origins.

Antoine should have never been in charge of the young boy and in fact, treated him severely. The following is an account found in the memoirs of Madame Campan, which sums up his treatment most accurately. He is addressed here as Capet:

Simon and his wife, cut off all those fair locks that had been his youthful glory and his mother's pride. This worthy pair stripped him of the mourning he wore for his father; and as they did so, they called it "playing at the game of the spoiled king." They alternately induced him to commit excesses, and then half starved him. They beat him mercilessly; nor was the treatment by night less brutal than that by day. As soon as the weary boy had sunk into his first profound sleep, they would loudly call him by name, "Capet! Capet!" Startled, nervous, bathed in perspiration, or sometimes trembling with cold, he would spring up, rush through the dark, and present himself at Simon's bedside, murmuring, tremblingly, "I am here, citizen."—"Come nearer; let me feel you." He would approach the bed as he was ordered, although he knew the treatment that awaited him. Simon would buffet him on the head, or kick him away, adding the remark, "Get to bed again, wolfs cub; I only wanted to know that you were safe." On one of these occasions, when the child had fallen half stunned upon his own miserable couch, and lay there groaning and faint with pain, Simon roared out with a laugh, "Suppose you were king, Capet, what would you do to me?" The child thought of his father's dying words, and said, "I would forgive you." (1)

Louis Charles never saw his mother again, and a year later she was executed. Antoine was long gone by this time, and the child was now kept in isolation, utterly neglected. A doctor was finally called in to attend him, and found him despondent in a filthy cell, covered in fleas. It was too late. At 10 years old, Louis Charles died from tuberculosis.

Rumors persisted for many years that Louis Charles had not died in prison, but had been secretly removed to someday regain his father's place as king. Many came forward claiming to be him, but in the end, it is believed that Louis Charles died in the Temple prison, alone and abandoned. His remains were dumped into a mass grave, but his heart was preserved. He was finally laid to rest next to his parents in the Basilica at St. Denis, a northern suburb of Paris, on June 8, 2004. (2)

Marie Thérèse Charlotte

Marie Thérèse Charlotte, also known as Madame Royale, was the first child of Louis and Marie born in December 1778, seven years into their marriage. She was absolutely adored by her parents, and although a son was most desired, her mother relished in the fact that a baby girl would be all her own. In the Historic Memoirs of Madame Campan, First Lady in Waiting to the Queen, Marie is quoted as saying,

> *Poor little one. You were not wished for, but you are not on that account less dear to me. A son would have been rather the property of the State. You shall be mine; you shall have my undivided care, shall share all my happiness, and console me in all my troubles.* (3)

Marie Thérèse certainly lived a privileged life as the princess, but her world changed drastically when the royal family was forcibly taken from Versailles to Paris where they would be imprisoned. Once the family was taken to the Temple Tower, her father was executed and later she was separated from her mother and brother. Although her treatment was not as harsh as Louis

Charles, she suffered greatly in mind and spirit. Eventually her aunt, Madame Elisabeth, her only companion at the time, was removed from their living quarters and later executed. From then on she led a lonely existence with only two books in her possession. Often, she could hear the cries and screams of her brother, but would never see him again.

Finally, as the revolution died down, Marie Thérèse was allowed to leave France for Austria. She lived in the court of Vienna and married, but had no children. She moved throughout Europe, even returning to France for a short time. She died of pneumonia in 1851 when she was 72 years old. (4)

Robespierre

Maximilien de Robespierre was born in Arras, France in 1758 and was raised by his grandparents. He went to college, became a lawyer, and later traveled to Paris and joined the political scene near the time of the revolution. He was known for defending the poorest of the poor and soon was called, "The Incorruptible," as he stuck diligently to a rigorous moral code.

Somewhere along the way he stretched his beliefs to an uncompromising level. He began to think that the end justifies the means, and whatever it took to elevate the rights of man over the rule of the French monarchy was morally acceptable. He became a member of the radical Jacobin group that operated outside the government. He became increasingly popular, although many thought he was too far-reaching in his zeal against the aristocracy.

Robespierre spoke with passion, convincing many that Louis XVI must die, so that the country might live. Once the king was executed, Robespierre became giddy with power. He helped initiate the Reign of Terror in the summer of 1793, a time where thousands of French citizens lost their lives, most by guillotine. In this, he was successful at purging most of his political adversaries and is quoted as saying, *Terror is nothing else than justice, prompt, severe, inflexible.*

Finally, the bloodbath ended, but not until Robespierre got his due. He became recognized as a madman, and in July the following year, he and many of his associates were arrested and put into prison. He managed to escape and hide in the Hôtel de Ville (City Hall), and through a botched suicide attempt, he injured his jaw. That night he and 21 of his followers were captured and arrested, and the following day put to death by the very instrument he used so freely, the guillotine. (5)

Louis XVI, King of France

Louis XVI was shy and awkward as a boy and later as a man. He did not possess the leadership skills, or the command he would need to lead his country through such tumultuous times. At the age of 20, when he was crowned king, France was in such financial upheaval that many believe nothing could have saved them. His great-great grandfather, Louis XIV, also known as The Sun King, had built Versailles, demanding such elegance that it was necessary to tax his subjects into poverty. Years later, Louis XV is quoted as saying,

"Aprois moi, le deluge." Meaning, "After me, the flood."

Louis' short-sighted outlook along with those of his predecessors would eventually cause the French monarchy to fall and never recover. Louis XVI never stood a chance.

A few years ago, I came across a website, *Eyewitness to History*. One particular section caught my eye. It was an account written by an English priest living in France, Henry Essex Edgeworth, whose memoirs were originally published in 1815. Edgeworth escorted King Louis XVI to his execution. I believe this account fully captures the king's character at his most vulnerable time. The guillotine is something none of us have ever witnessed, and hopefully never will. I feel this account describes the horrific scene in shocking detail.

The King, finding himself seated in the carriage, where he could neither speak to me nor be spoken to without witness, kept a profound silence. I presented him with my breviary, the only book I had with me, and he seemed to accept it with pleasure: he appeared anxious that I should point out to him the psalms that were most suited to his situation, and he recited them attentively with me. The gendarmes, without speaking, seemed astonished and confounded at the tranquil piety of their monarch, to whom they doubtless never had before approached so near.

The procession lasted almost two hours; the streets were lined with citizens, all armed, some with pikes and some with guns, and the carriage was surrounded by a body of troops, formed of the most desperate people of Paris. As another precaution, they had placed before the horses a number of drums, intended to drown any noise or murmur in favour of the King; but how could they be heard? Nobody appeared either at the doors or windows, and in the street nothing was to be seen, but armed citizens – citizens, all rushing towards the commission of a crime, which perhaps they detested in their hearts. The carriage proceeded thus in silence to the Place de Louis XV, and stopped in the middle of a large space that had been left round the scaffold: this space was surrounded with cannon, and beyond, an armed multitude extended as far as the eye could reach. As soon as the King perceived that the carriage stopped, he turned and whispered to me, "We are arrived, if I mistake not." My silence answered that we were. One of the guards came to open the carriage door, and the gendarmes would have jumped out, but the King stopped them, and leaning his arm on my knee, "Gentlemen," said he, with the tone of majesty, "I recommend to you this good man; take care that after my death no insult be offered to him – I charge you to prevent it."... As soon as the King had left the carriage, three guards surrounded him, and would have taken off his clothes, but he repulsed them with haughtiness – he undressed himself, untied his neckcloth, opened his shirt, and arranged it himself. The guards, whom the determined countenance of the King had for a moment disconcerted, seemed to recover their audacity. They surrounded him again, and would have seized his hands. "What are you attempting?" said the King, drawing back his hands. "To bind you," answered the wretches. "To bind me," said the King, with an indignant air. "No! I shall never consent to that: do what you have been ordered, but you shall never bind me..."

The path leading to the scaffold was extremely rough and difficult to pass; the King was obliged to lean on my arm, and from the slowness with which he proceeded, I feared for a moment that his courage might fail; but what was my astonishment, when arrived at the last step, I felt that he suddenly let go my arm, and I saw him cross with a firm foot the breadth of the whole scaffold; silence, by his look alone, fifteen or twenty drums that were placed opposite to me; and in a voice so loud, that it must have been heard it the Pont Tournant, I heard him pronounce distinctly these memorable words: "I die innocent of all the crimes laid to my charge; I Pardon those who have occasioned my death; and I pray to God that the blood you are going to shed may never be visited on France."

He was proceeding, when a man on horseback, in the national uniform, and with a ferocious cry, ordered the drums to beat. Many voices were at the same time heard encouraging the executioners. They seemed reanimated themselves, in seizing with violence the most virtuous of Kings, they dragged him under the axe of the guillotine, which with one stroke severed his head from his body. All this passed in a moment. The youngest of the guards, who seemed about eighteen, immediately seized the head, and showed it to the people as he walked round the scaffold; he accompanied this monstrous ceremony with the most atrocious and indecent gestures. At first an awful silence prevailed; at length some cries of "Vive la Republique!" were heard. By degrees the voices multiplied and in less than ten minutes this cry, a thousand times repeated became the universal shout of the multitude, and every hat was in the air. (6)

Queen Marie Antoinette

At the tender age of 14, a sheltered, shy, petite princess was escorted from her luxurious home in Vienna, Austria to France in a political move arranged by her mother. She was to immediately marry Louis XVI, age 15, in a lavish ceremony, thus cementing friendship between the two countries. From the moment Marie arrived at Versailles, she was an outsider and in some ways, would remain so until her death. Rumors swirled questioning her motives and her character from the moment she stepped out of the carriage that very first day.

Throughout her time as dauphine, and then queen, she tried countless times to please everybody, and thus, seemed to please no one. For whatever reason, perhaps boredom and a feeling of helplessness over her own existence, she became preoccupied with fashion, hairstyles, shoes, and jewelry. Her style was copied throughout Europe. This obsession came at great expense however, and in the end her extravagance would be another key part of her undoing.

Once the Royal family was imprisoned, Marie, in her thirties, tried valiantly to save the monarchy. It was all she ever knew and of course she wished to save her children's way of life and their heritage, but to no avail. Behind it all, I do not believe Marie was the power hungry, selfish, and uncaring person she was portrayed as in the end. At her core she was a wife and a mother, put into an impossible position with no real guidance or direction.

As with many human beings, her life was full of inconsistencies, but did she deserve such a tragic ending? Was she a horrible person, or was she living the life that had been set out for her, too naïve to see the changes coming until it was too late?

The following was written about her in 1893. I believe it sums her up well.

> *She was not a guilty woman, neither was she a saint; she was an upright, charming woman, a little frivolous, somewhat impulsive, but always pure; she was a queen, at times ardent in her fancies for her favourites and thoughtless in her policy, but proud and full of energy; a thorough woman in her winsome ways and tenderness of heart, until she became a martyr.* (7)

References

(1) (3) The Project Gutenberg. *Memoirs of The Court of Marie Antoinette, Queen of France, Complete, by Madame Campan*, Release Date: October 2, 2006 [EBook #3891], Last Updated: August 23, 2014

(2) Biography.com editors. April 1, 2014, *Louis XVII*: https://www.biography.com/people/louis-xvii-38095 (Retrieved Nov. 2017)

(4) Moniek. Oct. 7, 2016, *The Ruin of a Princess: Marie-Thérèse of France*: https://www.historyofroyalwomen.com/marie-therese-of-france-3/ruin-princess-marie-therese-france (Retrieved Nov. 2017)

(5) Biography.com editors. Nov. 9, 2014, *Maximilien de Robespierre*: https://www.biography.com/people/maximilien-de-robespierre-37422 (Retrieved Nov. 2017)

(6.1) Eyewitness to History. *The Execution of Louis XVI, 1793*: www.eyewitnesstohistory.com/louis.htm (1999) (Retrieved Nov. 2017)

(6.2) Cronin, Vincent. *Louis and Antoinette* (1975)

(6.3) Edgeworth, Henry in Thompson, J.M. (Ed.). *English Witnesses of the French Revolution* (1938, Memoirs originally published 1815).

(7) Maxime de La Rocheterie. *The Life of Marie Antoinette* (1893)

Acknowledgments

Writing a first novel can be quite daunting, and this one was no exception. I would like to thank the following people for endlessly supporting me throughout this process:

First, thanks to my parents, for always being my cheerleaders, raising me to not be afraid to try new things, and supporting me in all my endeavors.

Thanks to my friend Jeff Cope, who encouraged me to get this book off the shelf, dust it off, and work on it. He guided me through those first few difficult edits, and without him, this book would have never come to life.

I appreciate my daughter Meagan for editing one of the 'almost' final drafts and giving me great insight on how to make this a better book. Thanks also to my son Wes and daughter Lexi, who both showed great interest and encouragement throughout this process.

I owe a debt of gratitude to a few special friends that not only encourage me through life, but also as I wrote this book, namely Diane, Deanne, Anne, Dettye Ann and the Sistas.

I would also like to thank authors Jennifer L Scott, and Tracy Porter for helping me believe in myself as a new author, and answering my many questions.

Thanks to Val Perry and the Bloomingdale Regional Library in Valrico, Florida, for supporting new authors through the Life Story Writing Project.

Thank you to the organization National Novel Writing Month (nanowrimo.org). I used this platform to get my first draft on paper in 30 days. Without that deadline, this novel would've never been written.

To my precious YouTube followers... you people are the greatest! Once I announced I was working on this book, you all encouraged me to get it out there for all to read. Your excitement truly kept me going.

Thanks to Steve Alcorn at Writing Academy (writingacademy.com) for teaching me, answering my questions, and suggesting a great editor, Denise Gottshalk, to guide me through to my final draft. Thanks Denise.

Finally, to Mimi, my sweet friend in Paris... thank you for your marketing ideas and for your friendship.

Thank you for reading my novel! If you enjoyed it, would you mind leaving a review to recommend it to other readers? Thank you for your time.

Made in the USA
San Bernardino, CA
19 March 2018